The Whitman Kick

Also by Robert Burch

Queenie Peavy
Skinny
Simon and the Game of Chance
Two That Were Tough

PICTURE BOOKS:
The Jolly Witch
Joey's Cat

The WHITMAN KICK

by Robert Burch

E. P. Dutton | New York

Library of Congress Cataloging in Publication Data

Burch, Robert, date. The Whitman kick.

SUMMARY: Newly enlisted into the Army during World War II, a seventeen-year-old boy reminisces about his school days and his relationship with one special girl.
I. Title.
PZ7.B91585Wh [Fic] 77-23384 ISBN: 0-525-42677-9

Published in the United States by E. P. Dutton, a Division of Sequoia-Elsevier Publishing Company, Inc., New York

Published simultaneously in Canada by Clarke, Irwin & Company Limited, Toronto and Vancouver

Editor: Ann Durell Designer: Riki Levinson

Printed in the U.S.A. First Edition
10 9 8 7 6 5 4 3 2 1

The author and publisher gratefully acknowledge permission to quote the poetry appearing on the following pages:

page 12, two lines from "How Happy Is the Little Stone"
From POEMS by Emily Dickinson, Edited by Martha Dickinson Bianchi and Alfred Leete Hampson.

page 63, "New Love and Old"
Reprinted with permission of Macmillan Publishing Co., Inc. from COLLECTED POEMS by Sara Teasdale. Copyright 1915 by Macmillan Publishing Co., Inc., renewed 1943 by Mamie T. Wheless.

pages 72 and 73, "The Kiss"
Reprinted with permission of Macmillan Publishing Co., Inc. from COLLECTED POEMS by Sara Teasdale. Copyright 1911 by Sara Teasdale. Copyright 1922 by Macmillan Publishing Co., Inc.

page 73, six lines from "Child, Child"
Reprinted with permission of Macmillan Publishing Co., Inc. from COLLECTED POEMS by Sara Teasdale. Copyright 1917 by Macmillan Publishing Co., Inc., renewed 1945 by Maime T. Wheless.

for Sara and Claude Goza

Contents

1 Fresh Meat! 1
2 The Whitman Kick 7
3 Go Tell Buddy 16
4 Amanda's House 24
5 The Loving Couple 32
6 Prospects 38
7 The Plan 45
8 Gone with the Wind 53
9 Message from Buddy 60
10 Two Apart 67
11 The Doldrums 76
12 The Move 83
13 Voices in the Night 89
14 Amanda's Visit 93
15 Summer and Fall 101
16 The Return 107
17 Graduation and Gloria 112

1

Fresh Meat!

The kid from Macon is bragging. If he turns out to be as remarkable a soldier as he purports to have been a lover, World War II should not last much longer. He will win it for us with ease.

I am glad he is called the kid instead of me. At barely seventeen, it is likely that I am the youngest man in the barracks. Parental consent was required for me to enlist. Everyone else is eighteen or over. I let them think that I have been drafted too. I get by with it because I look older than I am. I have a dark, brooding look, someone once told me, and also, I am big for my age. The kid from Macon is neither tall nor short, and his coloring is so neutral that I could not say whether he is blond or brunet. Maybe he keeps us reminded of his sexual prowess lest we figure his life to have been as ordinary as his looks.

His story is over, and the ex-cop from Birmingham tells how he spent last weekend in the arms of an old girlfriend now living in Atlanta. Her husband had had the misfortune of being drafted earlier. "It was my farewell to freedom," says the ex-cop, "before reporting to this Godforsaken place.

I do not regard Fort McPherson as Godforsaken. Maybe that is because I have lived twenty miles from it all my life. On family outings when I was younger, my sisters and I looked forward to going past its front gates whenever we came to this part of Atlanta. The view from inside is not so exciting, but I do not hate it. No place within twenty miles of home is Godforsaken.

All of us in the barracks reported for duty on Monday. We have stood in lines all week and been given shots, uniforms, and orders to try to look like soldiers. At first we were called fresh meat by groups ahead of us in the lines. By now they have been shipped to training camps around the country, and we await our turn. In the meantime we yell "Fresh meat!" at new arrivals, we veterans of four days.

The guy we call Martin tells a story in which he makes a dumb mistake. At the end of it he looks at me and says, "I'll know better next time, won't I, Ponder?"

"You'll know!" I say.

Ponder is my last name. In the Army a first name is unnecessary except for identifying the last one. "Sound off with your first name and middle initial when your name is called," we are told often. "Alan J.," I yell on such occasions. I made up the J when I enlisted. A sergeant told me that without a middle name I should write NMI, the abbreviation for No Middle Initial, in filling out forms. I had rather be Alan J. Ponder than Alan NMI Ponder. Maybe later I will decide what the J stands for. I would have had no choice if birth certificates had been required in Ellenville when I was born. My arrival in the world was not recorded. "An excuse for being born," my sister Daisy once gave as the meaning of a birth certificate.

Daisy is my younger sister, and she is inclined to explain any word that has more than two syllables. At the end of May she finished the eighth grade. I finished the eleventh, graduating from high school. Twelfth grades, like birth certificates, are known in cities, but smaller communities do not always bother with them. I am glad Ellenville did not have another year of high school, or I might have had to endure it. I did not always dislike school, but last term was nothing to me. The only thing I will remember about my senior year is that the bombs fell on Pearl Harbor during it, and the world was shaken. My world had crumbled six months earlier.

"One more about Gloria!" someone is saying, and I realize that a story is expected of me. I tell about the first afternoon I drove Gloria home from Stumpy's, the lake and dance pavilion. Both of us were wearing swimsuits, and we parked on a trail back of the cemetery.

I am glad to have Gloria for my contribution to these sessions. Some of the stories I tell are true, and in them I get what I go after. With Gloria it was possible. If I had not known Gloria, I would have had to make her up. I could never talk about Amanda in an Army bull session.

The public-address system comes on, announcing visiting hours. "The following men have visitors in Lot K," says the speaker, and the names are called. Mine is one of them, and so is the ex-cop's. We walk to Lot K together. I hope that his visitor is his old girlfriend; I would like to see her. But his guest is an aunt from East Point, the Atlanta suburb where Fort McPherson is located, and my visitors are my father and Daisy.

"My goodness," says Daisy, disgustedly, "haven't they given you a rifle yet?"

Dad and I laugh. "Isn't it so?" he says. "What's the use of being in the Army if you don't get to tote around a gun!"

I explain to Daisy that I'll be given a rifle when I get to a training station. "Unless I'm assigned to an armored unit," I say, "in which case I suppose I'll be given a tank." Dad and I laugh again.

Our conversation remains light. Anything serious to be said to each other has been said already.

"We had a message from Buddy this afternoon," says Daisy. "A blue jay brought it."

"Oh, yeah? What was it?"

"It was for you. Buddy said tell you that you should have tried out for the Marines!"

All three of us laugh, and Dad says, "If you had told the Army doctors about Buddy, probably you'd have been excused from military service forever!"

"I'm sure of it!" I say. "They'd have known I was crazy!" Buddy is an imaginary character in a game that we have played for a long time. We invented him. Whenever a bird lights on the limb of holly just outside our den, we pretend that Buddy has sent it to tell us something. We make up the messages.

I give Daisy a message to send back to Buddy the next time she sees a blue jay on the holly branch. We are discussing it when visiting hours end.

The ex-cop and I head back to the barracks. His aunt brought him peanut brittle, which he shares with me. It makes up for his visitor not having been the girlfriend.

In the barracks the bull session is over. Some of the guys have gone to bed; others are sitting on their bunks, writing letters. I undress, take the towel from the end of my bunk, and tie it around me as I head for the shower. I return in time to crawl into the sack just as the lights go out.

I am not sleepy, but I do not mind turning in. It is my time with Amanda. No matter what happens during a day my thoughts at the end of it are always of her. The only dreams I care about are the ones I have when I'm awake. Asleep, they are apt to follow life and turn into nightmares. Awake, I steer them in the direction in which I wish life had gone.

Amanda and I had been special friends since we were in the sixth grade—which was the second year she had been in it. She had been kept out of school the previous term because of rheumatic fever, with complications. Until then she and my sister Irene had been in the same class, one grade ahead of me. The year that she dropped back I was on crutches, having broken both legs at the end of summer, showing off. I had climbed out on a high limb of the walnut tree in Lanky Turner's yard and jumped to the ground. Lanky and I had done it many times, always landing in a giant mound of straw we used to absorb the shock. This time I saw Rick Bledsoe across the road and yelled, "Hey, watch me!" I watched him to see if he was watching me instead of keeping my eyes on the mound of straw. I hit the flagstone walk.

When school started neither Amanda nor I was allowed to play any games that required moving about. We had to stay indoors, or sit at the edge of the playground, during recess and lunch period while our classmates had fun. At eleven I looked on girls as tiresome and made no effort to be friendly with Amanda. At twelve she looked on anyone eleven as a mere child and made no effort to be friendly with me. Soon we were fast friends. A bond developed between us so strong that by the next year, when we might have been able to join our classmates in some of their activities, we did not always bother.

In high school we continued to be content with each other. We were both stronger by then, although I still had a slight limp and could not take part in athletics till my final year—when I didn't really care whether I took part in anything. I got along fine with the boys in our class, and Amanda mixed with the girls, but we were closer to each other than to anyone else.

In thinking back I always stop at the spring of last year. Amanda and I were going into the homestretch of our junior year. She was seventeen after her birthday in February, and I would be sixteen in June. We were on what we called our Whitman Kick.

Amanda and I were both good students, and literature courses were our favorites. During all those months of forced inactivity we had turned into avid readers, and while we may not have understood poetry better than our friends, we were more interested in it. At times we even spoke to each other through the lines of some poet and knew exactly what the other meant. Or maybe we were avoiding direct confrontations that might have hurt. I regret that I was not more experienced—a bit older perhaps, and more daring—during the Whitman Kick.

2
The Whitman Kick

It is a drawing of two nudes, a man and a woman. Lin Davidson did it. Our school does not have an art department but Miss Cutter has turned fifth-period study hall into an art class for anyone who is interested. I'm not in it, but I have English sixth period with friends who are. We look at the picture while waiting for class to begin. "Miss Cutter thinks I have talent," says Lin.

"You mean she saw it?" asks Marie Bronson.

"Sure. We were told to do a quick sketch of the human figures. Of course, when she saw it, it was supposed to have been Adam and Eve in the Garden of Eden."

"It was so funny," says Sue Elkins. "Miss Cutter said, 'Now, students, if you'd like to see the human body treated with no trace of vulgarity, find time to look at Lin's drawing.' Then she went on around the room, stopping to see what everybody else was doing, and Lin changed Eve's face to look exactly like Miss Cutter's, and Adam suddenly became Mr. Goodwin!" Mr. Goodwin is our principal.

"Yeah, this takes talent," says Blake Rhodes. "Of one sort or another!" He hands the picture to Amanda, who asks Lin, "What would you have done if Miss Cutter had come back to you?"

"That's the advantage of charcoal," he says. "One swipe with an eraser and I could've smeared the evidence!"

The bell rings, and Mrs. Hatcher comes into the room. Amanda whispers, "Here, take it!" and I reach for the drawing. Some of our friends look to see if I can hide it quickly.

"All right!" says Mrs. Hatcher. "I can tell that something is being passed around—something you don't want me to see." Looking at Amanda she asks, "Do you know anything about it?"

"Oh, no, Mrs. Hatcher," says Amanda, smiling. I almost laugh aloud. Nobody can lie like Amanda.

While Mrs. Hatcher is asking Amanda if she is absolutely certain about it, I fold the drawing as if it's no more special than tomorrow's math assignment and reach over and put it in the open pocketbook beside Gloria Mason's desk. Gloria is busy writing a note and does not see what I have done. She is almost always busy writing a note to whatever boy interests her at the moment. Just now it is Hank Watkins.

"Very well," says Mrs. Hatcher, "if you'll give me your attention we'll get to the lesson for today. I'm sure that all of you have read the Whitman selections I assigned, and I hope some of you have looked up additional works of his. Suppose you tell me which poems you like best and why. And quote a few lines for the class, all right?" She gets out her roll book, which means that we'll be graded on our answers. "Rick Bledsoe, you may be first."

Rick is peering around, trying to figure out what I've done with Lin's drawing. He stammers, "Er . . . what was that, Mrs. Hatcher? I don't believe I quite understand the question."

"Maybe that's because you weren't listening." She puts a mark in her roll book—probably a zero—by Rick's name. "Alan, did you hear the question?"

"I like 'Beautiful Women,' " I answer, and everybody laughs.

Blake Rhodes looks back at me and whispers, "Doesn't everybody?" as I begin to quote: " '*Women sit or move to and fro, some old, some young, / The young are beautiful—but the old are more beautiful than the young.*' "

"Very good!" says Mrs. Hatcher, and she calls on other students. Most of them cite "O Captain! My Captain!" as their favorite poem, giving as reasons little more than "It rhymes" or "It's sad." But Amanda has a different one. She quotes: " '*When the lilac-scent was in the air and Fifth-month grass was growing, / Up this seashore in some briers, / Two feathered guests from Alabama, two together* . . .' " She stops there, her face turning red, and she looks at me. "I'm sorry, I didn't mean—"

"Why, that's lovely," says Mrs. Hatcher. "It's one of my favorites too, and *Fifth-month,* for any of you who don't know, refers to May."

It was to me instead of Mrs. Hatcher that Amanda had said she was sorry. We have been together so much that we can tell what the other is thinking. She fears that quoting lines with *Alabama, two together* in them somehow hurt me, but it has not. Town gossip has to do with my mother visiting a man in Alabama who is not my father—living with him, some say—but I am learning not to notice.

I look at Amanda and she understands. "Go on!" Mrs. Hatcher tells her.

Amanda brushes her hair back and continues: "I believe I'll skip the lines about the he-bird flying to and fro and the she-bird crouching on the nest and get to the part I really love." Then she says the lines so naturally that they seem her own instead of Walt Whitman's: " '*Shine! shine! shine! / Pour down your warmth, great sun! / While we bask, we two together. / Two together! / Winds blow south, or winds blow north, / Day come white, or night come black, / Home, or rivers and mountains from home, / Singing all time, minding no time, / While we two keep together.*' I like it," she says. "The poet seems to be talking to me. No, I'll change that: The poet is talking *for* me. I can't explain why, but it's the way I feel. I'd like to look at the sun and say exactly the same thing." So would I. And the two together are Amanda and me, not my mother and Dad's cousin, Tom Rockdale. The wind can blow south or north, and anything else can happen as long as Amanda is nearby.

"Yes, it's very beautiful," Mrs. Hatcher is saying, "but it too is sad. Listen to the next few lines after the love song about the two keeping together." She takes her book and reads: " '*Till of a sudden, / Maybe killed, unknown to her mate, / One forenoon the she-bird crouched not on the nest, / Nor returned that afternoon, nor the next, / Nor ever appeared again.*' " Closing the book, she asks Marie Bronson, "What do you think?"

"I don't think the she-bird should have gone off and got herself killed or whatever it was she got herself did. I mean, *done to.*"

"She got waylaid," I whisper.

"By a catbird!" says Blake.

Marie pays no attention to us. "I mean if she'd just stayed on the nest and let the he-bird bring worms and things to her, she'd have been better off."

"No doubt she would!" says Mrs. Hatcher, smiling. "And the world would have been deprived of the rest of that wonderful work." She begins to tell us how she feels about the entire poem, "Out of the Cradle Endlessly Rocking," and is still talking when the bell rings.

We return to homeroom and wait for the final bell. Amanda and I are at our desks, directly across from each other, when Gloria Mason comes down the aisle. As she goes by me I look down at her bag and ask, "Where'd you get that drawing?"

"What drawing?" asks Gloria, looking at the folded paper. When she discovers that it is Lin's artwork she says, "Why, you fiend!" and giggles as she drops it into my lap. "What if I'd been caught?"

Amanda asks, "What if you'd been caught at a lot of things?" They glare at each other till Amanda smiles as if she has not meant anything by the remark. Then the bell rings, and school is out. Lin claims his drawing, and Amanda and I walk to the drugstore. Instead of joining our friends there, we buy Cokes in paper cups and leave.

Hap Jordan and my sister Irene are parked in front of the drugstore, licking ice-cream cones.

"Want a ride home?" calls Hap.

"No, thanks," I say. "We'll walk." We live only two blocks away.

"Daisy's at her music lesson," calls Irene. "We'll pick her up in an hour."

Instead of answering I look back and nod. Then Amanda and I go home. We usually go to our house to listen to records and study for the next day—or to visit, if we don't have homework. Sometimes we go to Amanda's, but her house is not as pleasant, although it's a much nicer one than ours. Her mother is more interested in keeping the furnishings, including a collection of expensive figurines, polished and dusted than in having Amanda there. She has never objected to Amanda going home with me. Amanda says it cuts down on the chances of her mother's ornaments being accidentally broken.

At our house nobody worries about anything getting broken. It's an old house, and so is 'most everything in it. It was my father's homeplace, and about all that can be said for it is that we have plenty of room. My mother used to say that we also had ghosts. When she and Dad married, they moved here, and she looked after my grandmother and my great-uncle, both of whom were ill and very demanding. Last year my mother wanted to build a new house across town when Dad sold the lot next to us, especially after a filling station was put on it. But she could not convince him that we needed, or could afford, to move.

In the sitting room upstairs Amanda and I finish our homework. My sisters have not arrived home yet. Amanda closes her book and says, "There must be something wrong with me. I like Whitman better than Emily Dickinson."

"So do I," I say, turning up the record player.

"Yeah, but you're a boy." She quotes from a Dickinson poem: " '*How happy is the little stone / That rambles in the road alone*,' " and says, "I'd rather read about two together than a stone alone."

A sparrow lights on the holly branch outside the window, and I point at it. "A message from Buddy."

"Good!" says Amanda. "What is it?"

"Buddy says tell you that you shouldn't accuse Gloria of having hot pants!" We both laugh. "Buddy says that Gloria is blessed with a loving nature."

"She's blessed!" says Amanda. "What sort of message will you send back? The bird's waiting."

"You can reply. The messenger's a sparrow." It's one of the rules: Anybody can talk to sparrows. Some birds are for family members only, and certain species are for certain ones of us. The game is complicated, but we have been inventing it for six years.

"Very well!" says Amanda, looking at the sparrow. "Go tell Buddy that if he'll come out of hiding, Gloria'll give him a date and anything else he wants." She taps the window and the bird flies away.

"That's bad luck," I say.

"But I've heard you send him sassy messages."

"It's bad luck to shoo away one of his messengers."

"I think you made that up."

"Yes," I admit, "a long time ago."

"No, I think you made it up just now. You've never told me it was bad luck."

"Well, it is," I say, "whether I told you or not. Buddy'll get even." We look at each other as if we are deadly serious. Then I laugh, and Amanda smiles. After all, it is only a game.

"Do you suppose Gloria goes all the way with every boy she dates?" asks Amanda.

"If she doesn't, it's probably not because her dates don't try. Her boyfriends are usually the fast movers; at least, most of 'em like to leave the impression that they are."

"Why do you boys go for that?"

"Go for what?"

"For letting Gloria make the decisions. All she has to do is snap her fingers when she's ready for a new boyfriend, and whoever she's selected comes running."

"Aw, everybody knows she's fickle and that it won't last. But she's so cute and pretty that I guess you're right. She can just about get anybody she wants."

Amanda looks at me. "I didn't know you thought she was all that pretty."

"How could anybody with eyes not notice?"

"Even so, I somehow hadn't thought you looked at girls that way. And Gloria is not all that cute. Her sweater may be filled out, but her head's empty, if you ask me, and if that's what you call cute then I don't trust your judgment!" Amanda is getting mad. "And besides, one of these days she'll get pregnant, and 'cute Gloria' will have had so many boyfriends that poor old Dr. Mason won't know where to aim the shotgun!"

I laugh, thinking of Gloria's father. He retired early from dental practice, some say because of a drinking problem. For whatever reason, he appears unsteady, and the thought of him aiming a gun is funny to me. "Don't worry," I say. "Dr. Mason is not the shotgun type. If the occasion arises he'll ask the sheriff to round up a firing squad. Then every boy who's had anything to do with Gloria will be lined up and shot through the head! Does that make you feel better?"

"I've got to go," says Amanda, gathering up her books. At the door, she turns back and asks, "Have you ever looked at me?"

I'm surprised. Of course I've looked at her. I've watched her turn from a thin, sickly young girl into a healthy, older one—although she still has to be careful because of the heart damage when she was ill. She has never seemed to care much about the way she looks, not fixing up the way some girls do, and she wears clothes that are not frilly. Her skin and eyes are so pretty that she doesn't need makeup to help them, and her hair, a rich, dark brown, has a bit of curl in it and looks good without any special styling. She is what I suppose is called a natural beauty; I've never really thought about it. "Sure, I've looked at you. Why?"

"I mean in the way you must have looked at Gloria?" She smiles. "What would you do if I took off my blouse right now?"

I ask, "What would you do if I took off my pants?"

"Take them off and see," she says, and we look at each other for a moment. I'm excited and scared at the same time, knowing that if I take a step toward her she will not back away. But I do not move. Then she laughs again, and I laugh with her as if we have made one of our jokes.

"I'll see you tomorrow," she says, going from the room and down the stairs while I put another record on the player.

"Yeah," I call as she opens the front door. "See you tomorrow."

3

Go Tell Buddy

"Go tell Buddy that it's sad but true: We're no good." I say it to a towhee on the holly limb.

Daisy corrects me. "Alice didn't say we're no good. She said we've gone to seed."

The towhee cocks its head at a funny angle. "Not bird seed, you dumbbell!" I say, and it flies away as if it is offended. Then I ask Daisy, "Why does Alice think we're down and out? 'Cause Mom ran off and left us?"

Daisy turns to me angrily. "Mom has not run off and left us!"

"She has so."

"Our mother is visiting in Montgomery, Alabama," says Daisy, as if she is explaining the situation to an outsider.

"Three months is a long time to stay off visiting."

"Dad says she'll come back sooner or later, and that everybody will 'forgive and forget,' and things'll be the same as they always were."

"I won't forgive," I say bitterly. "And I won't forget."

Maybe it is because I have loved my mother so much in earlier years that I have gone to the other extreme now. I hate her, although I know that love and forgiveness should go together. With me they do not.

"Well, anyway," says Daisy. "We weren't talking about Mom, not in the beginning. It was just after recess, and Mrs. Hill was talking about changes and progress, and Alice said my family wasn't very progressive. She said that her father said my father wasn't a shrewd businessman or he wouldn't have sold the lot next to our house to ol' Doc Swanson so he could turn around and sell it to an oil company for a big profit. She says that her father said anybody but Dad would have sold it directly to an oil company in the first place. It being on a corner and almost in the middle of town, she said her father said Dad should have known how desirable it was for a commercial location." Daisy catches her breath and explains, "That means a place for business."

"No kidding!" I say. "Well, Dad's not greedy. Anyway, he sold the lot to Doc Swanson for him to build a house to live in; that's what he said he was going to do with it."

"That's what I told the class," says Daisy. "I said Dad was too trusting, and it was then that Grady Maxwell said, yeah, he was too trusting all right, and where did we think Mom was now."

"What'd you say?"

"Nothing. Mrs. Hill told Grady that we shouldn't get personal."

I am silent, and Daisy stares out the window that overlooks the grease rack of the filling station. After a moment she says, "But it is a sin and a shame about that tacky station and—"

I interrupt her. "Wait! I've just read an article about

southern speech. It seems we give ourselves away by the words and expressions we use as well as our accent."

"I don't mind anyone knowing I'm a southerner," protests Daisy. "Especially when everybody else in Ellenville is too."

"I don't either," I say. "But I don't care for some of the things we've worked to death. According to the article, *tacky* is still overused by southern belles, but *kissing kin* is less popular than it once was."

The door opens suddenly and Irene comes in. "Did somebody call me?" she asks. Putting on the exaggerated drawl she uses whenever she imitates anyone who imitates southerners, and swishing her hips as if they are swinging a hoop skirt back and forth, she says, "Alan, honey-chile, and deah sweet sistah Daisy, I thought to my soul I heard someone say 'southern belle.' "

We laugh, and Daisy says, "If they ever do *Gone with the Wind* over, you ought to play the part of Scarlett."

"I intend to!" says Irene, batting her eyelashes. Then she becomes serious. "What's all this about us being washed up? I couldn't help hearing. I was in my room brooding over algebra—which, by the way, means miserable mathematics that may keep me from graduating—and your conversation was more interesting. So I decided to quit eavesdropping and join you."

"Well," explains Daisy, "at school today Mrs. Hill was talking about the changes in the times and how the Depression is over and Tray County was agricultural—that means farming—for such a long time, but gradually it's gotten more houses and fewer farms till now it's mostly residential. That means where folks live."

"I'd never have guessed!" says Irene.

"According to her, someday you won't be able to tell where Atlanta leaves off and Ellenville begins. And then we talked about old houses in the middle of town that have been demolished."

She pauses to explain the word, but I beat her to it: "That means torn down."

"Yes," she agrees, "and we talked about how this part of town is growing, with new stores and all. Then about that time Mrs. Hill was called to the office, and she said for Nelda Hanson to pretend to be the teacher and for us to continue with our discussion. She lets us take turns being the teacher when she has to be out of the room."

"That's a mistake on her part!" I say.

Daisy continues. "Nelda went to the front of the room, and the first thing she said was that our house hasn't been torn down and that it's in the middle of town. Her folks told her, she said, how once upon a time our house was one of the nicest places around here. She said that her mother says it makes her plain sick because it hasn't been kept up and that now it's sitting side by side with a filling station."

"We were here before the filling station," I say.

"Eddy Shore said it was our house that made the filling station look bad."

Irene laughs. "Well, don't let what people say bother you. Try telling them that maybe we like living here. Why, until recently I could look out my window at night and all I'd see would be the stars and the moon and clouds drifting by. But nowadays, wow! I can see a neon light blinking on and off that says ECONOMY GASOLINE, THE BEST BARGAIN IN TOWN."

I help Irene with her act: "And tell them that while the

moon was on a most irregular schedule and on some nights didn't shine at all, the sign that says ECONOMY GASOLINE has not failed us yet!"

"Oh, nobody's ever serious around here."

Irene glances out the window that overlooks the station. "And, anyway, if Buddy doesn't mind, why should we?"

"That's another thing," complains Daisy. "All my friends think we're crazy to play a silly pretend-game about something that doesn't exist."

"Then they're not your friends," I say, "And besides, the game is not pretend, it's Buddy who is."

"They say, 'Well, what is Buddy? If he's not a person, then he must be a troll, or a fairy, or an elf,' and I tell them we didn't get around to making up exactly what he is, that it's just a stupid game we play."

The game started the year I had the measles. One day while I was in bed my mother had motioned toward the holly tree. "See the redbird? It brought you a message to hurry and get well!"

I had not looked up. I was angry that I had become ill in spring just when it was time to start baseball practice. But at noon, when Mom had brought my lunch, there was raisin-pecan pie for dessert. I knew she had made it especially for me, but instead of thanking her I asked, "Who sent the message?"

"What message?"

"The one by the bluebird."

"No, it was a redbird." Mom had smiled. "If it had been a bluebird I wouldn't have known what it said. I've never been able to understand a word a bluebird says."

My mother has a lively imagination. Maybe I do also, which is not necessarily a blessing—but it comes in handy sometimes. In years past, during family read-aloud sessions we occasionally stopped in the middle of a story and let everyone try to make up an ending. Mom and I were better at it than Irene, Daisy, or Dad. "You're too much alike," Dad used to tell us. Sometimes we made up an ending that everybody liked so well we'd decide not to read the rest of the story—lest the real ending disappoint us.

In appearance my mother and I are also very much alike. Both of us are dark. My sisters favor Dad: They're nice-looking, sandy-haired types. They and Dad have what an elderly, outspoken relative once described as open faces. She said anyone could tell at a glance what they were thinking, but that no one could possibly guess what was on the mind of my mother or me by looking at us. She said we could appear to be melancholy one second and outrageously happy the next. According to her, our smiles were so flashy they could be turned on and off like electric lights. "But who sent the message by the redbird?" I had asked again, that day six years ago, and Mom had answered, "Oh, somebody."

"Somebody or some buddy?"

She had laughed. "Yes, of course, that was it! Some buddy. A buddy to the birds!"

"Where does he live?"

Mom had looked out the window into the wooded lot that would eventually be cleared for the filling station. "There near those dogwoods, that's where Buddy lives. My redbird friend didn't explain what sort of creature he is, but I suppose it's enough for us to know that someone out there is thinking of us."

"Maybe he'll send other messages," I had said, and the game was under way. It had been fun to watch for birds. If they lit on the limb outside the window they were messengers, and a message had to be made up. Mom had continued to insist that she and bluebirds did not speak the same language, so one of our rules was that I had to take all messages from that species. Soon the whole family was playing. Even when I was able to be out of bed, and what we had called the sick room was turned into the combination play and study area that it is now, Buddy had not been abandoned.

A towhee, perhaps the same one that was here a while ago, lights in the tree. I look at it and say for Daisy's benefit, "Go tell Buddy he's an embarrassment to us all, and for him to quit sending messages over here." When the bird does not fly away, I add: "Tell him to borrow the key to the men's room of the filling station and go flush himself down the toilet!" Irene and I laugh, but Daisy does not.

"What message did Buddy send by the towhee?" asks Irene. Towhees always bring complaints.

"He said tell us that our lawn is a disgrace!" Although it is late winter, the last of the leaves from fall are still on the ground. "He said tell us that he doesn't see why Daisy can't rake leaves all day Saturday so that our run-down old house will at least have a clean yard."

"Oh, you act like everything's funny," says Daisy, and then she shouts, "But it's not!" She sniffs back tears and runs to her room.

"I didn't mean to make her cry," I say.

"She needs a good cry," says Irene. "If she held herself together while the seventh grade was working us over, then she's earned the right to let go now."

On the record player "Jersey Bounce" is repeating itself

for the third time. Irene stops it, puts on "Blues in the Night," and sits down to listen. "We'll give Daisy a few minutes," she says. "Then I'll go talk to her before I start supper."

"She'll have to realize that we're now considered fair game for gossip," I say.

"Of course, not all of it is gossip," says Irene, looking so worried that I wish she'd go back to being Scarlett O'Hara.

4

Amanda's House

Amanda's mother is almost always at home. The Housekeeper, Amanda and Ellie call her. Ellie is Amanda's sister, away at college.

Amanda leads me across the front porch, and we wait for her mother to open the door. After school we tried to study at our house, but Daisy and two of her friends were there, so we decided to leave.

Amanda's mother unlocks the front door, and we go inside. She says, "Oh, it's you!" to Amanda. She does not say anything to me.

I put Amanda's books on a small table in the foyer, but her mother says, "Clara just waxed that today." Clara is their maid.

Amanda starts to gather up the books, and I sit down on a small bench to tie a shoelace. It has been untied since noon and does not worry me, but tying it gives me something to do.

"The upholstering on that love seat is brand-new," says Mrs. Moore, and I hop up. I swat at the cream-colored cushion as if I may have left some trace of dirt on it. I am reasonably clean, but Mrs. Moore looks at me as if I am a pile of manure. I edge away from the cream-colored love seat lest it reach out and hit me for having sat on it.

We follow Mrs. Moore through the living room, careful to walk on a stretch of brown paper that is a path across the floor. The pale green carpeting is supposed to bring out the subtle colors of the Portuguese tiles in the fireplace and show off the porcelains to advantage. It also shows off footprints, although I doubt that many have ever been on it. Amanda says that the brown paper is taken away only when the Ellenville Women's Club meets with her mother.

"Where've you been?" asks Mrs. Moore, stopping in the dining room to rearrange china in the breakfront. It is her current project.

"Three guesses!" says Amanda, and she and I prop ourselves on the back of dining chairs.

"I'd say you've been at the Ponders', studying with Alan."

"Hooray!" says Amanda. "You win the prize!" She picks up a porcelain figurine from the corner cupboard and motions as if she is going to toss it to her mother. "Catch!"

"NOOOOOO!" screams her mother, and when Amanda places the figurine back on the shelf, Mrs. Moore puts her hands to her head and leans over as if she may collapse. "You'll be the death of me yet. Don't you know that's—"

Amanda interrupts. "Yes, I know! It's the Balloon Pedlar by Royal Doulton, and it cost lots of money and is so fragile it will shatter to smithereens if it isn't handled with loving care."

Mrs. Moore turns back to the breakfront. After moving a cream pitcher and sugar dish from one shelf to another she stands back to study them. Behind her, Amanda pretends to swat the Balloon Pedlar with the back of her hand, looking as if she would like to knock it across the room.

"I knew you were at the Ponders', of course," says Mrs. Moore, her voice a bit shaky. She has not recuperated from having seen a piece of her porcelain treated irreverently. "But I wish you'd make new friends."

Amanda has told me that her mother says this every now and then but that she has never insisted on it. Having Amanda somewhere else is better than having her here, according to Amanda. If she were at home more of the time she might really break something or walk on the carpeting.

Amanda turns the figurine around, pretending to study it. I wonder if she will push it to the edge of the shelf, the way she did one last summer. Then, if anyone brushes against it even slightly it will topple, the way the one had that Ellie broke. Amanda swears that she hadn't meant for Ellie to break it; she had just felt that *someone* should.

Mrs. Moore says, "I'm really serious this time. I think you should not stay at the Ponders' so much, and I'm glad to have a chance to discuss it with you and Alan." Suddenly she is including me in the conversation. "I've been criticized, I know, for letting you two run together the way you have, but after all, you've been close since you were in elementary school. You're more like brother and sister, I suppose." Amanda starts to say something, but her mother is not finished. She goes back to talking to Amanda only. "I think you should give up Alan and spend more time with girls your age, and maybe cultivate a new boyfriend or two and begin having real dates. When Ellie was your age, she was having dates regularly, and I see no reason why you wouldn't want to do the same thing." Amanda and I go to ball games together, usually with Dad and Daisy—and Mom, before she went away—and school programs that are held at night, and to Atlanta to a movie whenever anybody will take us. Otherwise, we do not have dates. Occasionally I see her on a Saturday or Sunday, but I do not have my driver's license yet, so we can't drive anywhere.

When her mother finishes Amanda says slowly, as if she is making an announcement that must be clearly understood: "Alan is not like a brother to me."

"Good!" says Mrs. Moore, putting a cake plate back into the breakfront. "Then you won't mind giving him up."

"Whatever makes you think that? My world would be over if I gave up Alan."

"He's a year younger than you are," Mrs. Moore reminds her. "And girls mature earlier than boys. You really would enjoy getting to know boys your own age or maybe a year or two older."

"Have you taken a good look at Alan recently?" asks Amanda. "Step out here, son!" she says, and I step over to where she is standing. "Now hold your shoulders back. Say, that's a good boy! Take a deep breath and try to look all grown up for the lady!" She and I laugh, but Mrs. Moore does not smile. Then Amanda says to her mother, "If he looked any more mature I'd die. And he's pretty, besides!"

"I dislike arguing with you," says Mrs. Moore, "and certainly Alan is handsome indeed. It's not on account of his looks that I think it best you cultivate other friends."

Suddenly it occurs to me what it is on account of, and I blurt out, "It's because of my mother, isn't it?"

I take her by surprise, and she answers, "Yes. Yes, it is."

Amanda stiffens. Sounding like Daisy explaining the situation, she says, "Mrs. Ponder is visiting her cousin in Alabama."

"Montgomery, Alabama," says Mrs. Moore, as if it makes a difference where in Alabama she is visiting. "And he is not her cousin, is he, Alan?"

"He's my father's cousin."

"They're old friends," says Amanda. "Like brother and sister. And it was the cousin who introduced Mr. and Mrs. Ponder to each other for the first time."

"I've heard she was engaged to the cousin then," says Mrs. Moore.

It strikes me that Amanda or I should say, "Yes, we are embarrassed by what's happening, but we can't help it." In recent weeks Amanda and I have talked about it, and we *are* embarrassed, but she does not admit it to her mother. "Mrs. Ponder went to Alabama to visit the cousin and his sister. His sister had been keeping house for him after his wife died, but she got sick and Mrs. Ponder is helping both of them."

Mrs. Moore, putting away small plates with cherries painted on them, says, "The sister has been in a convalescent home for the past two months." She sounds as if that settles it, that Amanda will rush out and start spending her time with girls her age or maybe entice some boy who already has his driver's license into taking an interest in her. Then she can play the part of her sister, Popular Ellie.

I can tell from the look in Amanda's eyes that she hasn't finished. In a softer tone she says, "I'm sorry Mrs. Ponder is away." She pats the Balloon Pedlar as if she's trying to make amends for almost smashing it. "At least when she was at home she acted as if she loved Mr. Ponder."

"Just what are you insinuating?" asks Mrs. Moore. "I have never so much as looked at another man since I married your father."

Amanda laughs. "I don't think you've looked at him! And I don't think you love anything except this house and the porcelains and the Ming vases and all your fine trappings." Her mother glares at her coldly, and Amanda says calmly, "I don't think you give a damn about anything else."

"You brat!" screams Mrs. Moore, swinging her right arm. She strikes Amanda across the cheek with the back of her hand in exactly the way Amanda had almost struck the Balloon Pedlar. Quickly Mrs. Moore says, "Oh, forgive me! I've never hit one of my children in my life, and I'm sorry. Please forgive me!"

Amanda looks at her coldly, then her eyes soften. "Of course I'll forgive you. I'll forgive you if you'll forgive me. Fair enough?"

Amanda and I go to the den and listen to her new recording of "I Don't Want To Set the World on Fire." Then she puts three different versions of "Stardust" on the player and goes out of the room. When she returns she tells me that I am invited to stay for supper. I've seldom been asked to eat with the Moores, and I do not think I should accept now. But Amanda says I must not leave her.

We decide to do our homework to "Stardust" only. Each time the three records are finished, one of us starts them over. When Mr. Moore arrives home the record player is turned off because he does not like it. We chat for a few minutes, and then Amanda asks him, "What about an advance on next week's allowance? I'm in urgent need of it!"

Mr. Moore smiles. "No doubt you are! But no, I think you have enough records."

"It's not for records," she says. "I want a pair of dark glasses like all the other girls are wearing. They're a new kind. Can't I have them?"

At that, Mr. Moore goes into a lecture about young people not appreciating the things they have, and how hard he has had to struggle to get where he is. He says Amanda must learn the value of a dollar. He is still lecturing when we are called to supper.

After the blessing, Amanda gets up to bring hot rolls from the kitchen. She starts to serve them in an elegant silver tray, but her mother stops her. "Take that back and bring the plated tray we always use."

"But things ought to be for enjoying," insists Amanda. "And besides, we have company!"

"Take it back!" orders her mother again, and Amanda looks at her father as if he will at least say, "I agree with Amanda. Why can't we use some of the finery around here?" But he doesn't say it. The tray is swapped for the other one, and there is a strained atmosphere during the rest of the meal. Amanda has told me that her father never crosses her mother about anything in the house—the expensive ornaments, the furniture, or their two daughters. They are hers to manage as she pleases; he earns the money to pay the bills. Industrious Dad, Amanda and Ellie call him.

When supper is over he says that he must go back to the office. As he starts out he hands Amanda a ten-dollar bill—much more than she had wanted before supper. "Buy the dark glasses," he says. It is his way of saying that he is sorry he lacked the guts to disagree with his wife. If he had pounded the table with his fist at supper and said, "We will use the silver tray!" it would have saved him ten dollars.

Amanda thanks him for the gift, but when he has gone she looks at the bill disgustedly. I know that to her it symbolizes the only kind of support he has ever given her.

I think no more about the money, but several days later she still has not bought the dark glasses. Then one morning during homeroom, Mrs. Rogers suggests that we send a gift to Ned James, a classmate who has been hurt in an automobile accident. He is in an Atlanta hospital. Handing a brown paper sack to Sue Elkins on the front row, Mrs. Rogers says, "Pass this around while I'm checking the roll, and if any of you want to make a donation we'll see what we can send Ned."

While she is calling names there is the usual commotion caused by late arrivals, and little attention is paid the brown bag as it is handed around the room. Most of us put a quarter or a couple of dimes or some nickels into it. But when the coins are emptied onto Mrs. Rogers' desk, there is a ten-dollar bill among them. With us, ten dollars is big money, and everyone wonders if the bill has been contributed by mistake. But no one admits to having given it, and Amanda, along with several other girls, wonders aloud who could have been so generous. She is, after all, a splendid liar.

5

The Loving Couple

We hear Dad calling from the foot of the stairs. I lower the volume on the record player and step into the hall. "What'd you say?" I ask.

"I said, 'Couldn't you turn down that record player?' "

"I just did."

Dad laughs. "I don't see how you and Amanda can study with all the noise."

"We've finished studying. We're just sitting quietly, reflecting on the day's misdeeds and thinking on the morrow."

Dad laughs again. "That's what I thought you were doing! Is Daisy with you?"

"She's in her room," I say, expecting her to open her door, but when she doesn't I ask, "Is there something you want her to do? I'll call her."

"No, it's all right." He leans out the front door for the *Atlanta Journal,* which has just hit the porch, and returns to the sitting room. This is his afternoon off. The appliance store where he works closes at noon every Wednesday.

I go back into the upstairs room. We call it the upstairs room as if it is the only one on the second floor, but in addition, my sisters and I each have a bedroom there. Amanda sits by the window, looking out. A big bird is circling in the distance. Pointing toward it I say, " '*The spotted hawk swoops by and accuses me.*' " It is the opening of a poem we learned when we first discovered Whitman.

"Yes," says Amanda, shaking her fist at the bird. " '*I too am not a bit tamed, I too am untranslatable, / I sound my barbaric yawp over the roofs of the world.*' "

"Say you do?" I tease, and then I quote more of the lines until she takes up where I leave off, sounding as if she is merely chatting with me: " '*I bequeath myself to the dirt to grow from the grass I love, / If you want me again look for me under your boot-soles.*' "

"That's an odd place to look!" I say as Amanda continues: " '*You will hardly know what I am or what I mean, / But I shall be good health to you. . . .*' " Then she skips to the last verse, saying it softly: " '*Failing to find me at first keep encouraged, / Missing me one place search another, / I stop somewhere waiting for you.*' "

I am strangely moved by the lines and her delivery of them, but instead of saying so, I correct her: "It's '*Failing to* fetch *me at first,*' not *find.*"

"Walt Whitman wouldn't care if I changed one of his words," she says, as if she and he were old pals. "It's amazing, isn't it, that a man so long ago could have written something that I can say to you right now, this very minute, and mean every word! I don't understand why everybody in the world doesn't love poetry."

I feel like saying, "Everybody in the world *would* love

poetry if they could hear you recite it," but instead I stare at a sparrow perched on a telephone wire. Amanda sees it, too. "Oh, good!" she says. "Maybe it'll fly over here." A second sparrow flies toward it.

"Were you expecting a message?" I ask.

"Who knows?" she says, just as the first bird flies to a branch of the holly tree.

"I'll take the message," says Amanda.

"What is it?"

"It's a sparrow."

"Of course it's a sparrow. I can see that for myself. But what's the message?"

"It's for me," she says, sounding as if it has been a telephone call and is strictly personal.

"Buddy's messages are always shared," I insist. "He doesn't mind who hears them."

"Oh, all right. The message was that you and I should end our friendship at once."

I look at her, puzzled. "But you shall be good health to me! Remember?"

"Yes, I know."

"Do you want to end our 'friendship'?"

Amanda shrugs. "It was Buddy who sent the message, not me."

I cannot question her. It is one of the rules: After a message has been made up, the person receiving it may flatly refuse to have any idea about what Buddy meant. Mom made up that rule, and there have been times when it has added interest to the game. Amanda and I have called it the fifth amendment since reading about court trials in which defendants refused to answer questions on the grounds that they might incriminate themselves. Their right to do this is guaranteed by the Fifth Amendment of the Constitution, but I wish now we had not adopted it for our game. I want to know if Amanda's parents are putting real pressure on her to spend less time with me. The term *friendship* has surprised me almost as much as the message itself. I have never thought of it. I suppose it is a friendship, certainly we've been friends for a long time. But we've never referred to our relationship as a friendship. On the other hand, we haven't spoken of it as a romance either. In fact, we've never spoken of it. "What sort of answer are you going to send back?" I ask.

"I'm thinking," she says.

Just then the other sparrow flies from the telephone wire toward the house. It swoops down and mounts the one that is already on the holly limb, fluttering its wings to keep its balance while the mating act takes place.

I laugh. "Well, you can forget the return message. These sparrows aren't going to take a reply back to Buddy."

"Don't birds always take him a message?"

"Any bird involved in a sex scandal is disqualified." I sound like an official in a ball game quoting regulations.

"Is that a rule?"

"Yes, I made it up just then. It's the first time the occasion has arisen!"

We both laugh, but Amanda protests: "It was not a sex scandal. It was the natural act of a loving couple. But maybe you're right; the messenger has other things to do, anyway."

"Absolutely!" I say, leaning over her shoulder to look at the two sparrows. "The he-bird and the she-bird better go build a nest instead of hopping around out there like they've lost their senses."

Amanda looks up at me and smiles. Her face is directly underneath mine. For a moment neither of us says anything; then she lifts her head higher. Our lips meet and we kiss. She stands up, and my arms go around her, pulling her closer to me. Her arms are over my shoulders, pressing tightly, when Dad calls from the foot of the stairs, "Alan, are you there?"

I hope that I have not heard him, that he has not called. Amanda and I hold each other closer. Dad yells, "I say up there, anybody home?"

I move away from Amanda. "I'm here," I answer. "I mean, we're here."

"I'm going to ride around a bit before suppertime," he says.

At that, Daisy pops out of her room. "I want to go with you," she says. Earlier, when he had inquired about her as though he might have a chore to be done, she had not heard. I do not blame Daisy for hearing only what she wants to hear.

"Sure," says Dad, "I want you to go with me. Alan, you and Amanda come ride with us, too."

"Er, no, thanks, Dad. We've got some studying to do."

"You said a while ago that you'd finished."

"We were, er . . . forgetting geometry. That's it, we slap forgot about geometry."

"Well, maybe you'd better slap forget about it till tonight and come ride with us. We'll look at the new houses going up across town and then drop Amanda off on our way back."

I know there is no way out. My father doesn't want to leave Amanda and me in the house alone. In years past nobody minded how much time we spent with each other.

We had studied, worked crossword puzzles, popped corn, played Monopoly and other games by ourselves, and nobody cared. Of course, Mom was with us then, but often she had gone visiting or shopping, leaving the two of us together. But recently I have sensed that Dad doesn't think we should be here unless someone else in the family is at home, too. Now, all of a sudden, I have an uneasy feeling that he is right. In a way I am glad that Amanda and I are not to be left alone. I don't know why; I don't understand my own feelings. At the same time, the excitement of having been so close to her in this new way is almost uncontrollable.

I turn to Amanda, "We'll have to go." She starts from the room, but I hang back a moment to try to settle down. I think of winter rains, sleet storms, and showering in ice water—anything except the warmth of Amanda's body next to mine.

6

Prospects

"Do you think we might really buy a house over in that new section?" asks Daisy.

"Well, I don't know," says Dad, wiping the dishes after I wash them. The menfolks, as Dad calls himself and me, do the dishes at night, and the ladies, Irene and Daisy, cook the supper. Miriam, the hired woman, comes during the day and does the rest of the cooking and the house-cleaning, but she has threatened to quit unless the kitchen is clean when she comes to work every morning. After Mom left, Dad decided that it would not be fair to expect Irene, with Daisy's help, to prepare supper and wash up afterwards. So he volunteered his services—and mine too.

I turn on the tap to add hot water to the dishpan that is used for rinsing. The single basin in the sink is filled with soapy water, and I must hold the dishpan while filling it. "If we buy a new house," I say, "it had better have a double sink!"

"Yes, sirree," says Dad, winking at Daisy. "It had sure better!" Daisy is sitting at the kitchen table. It gives her pleasure to visit in the kitchen when there is no risk of being asked to help with the work.

I don't really mind helping, but I like to complain about it. The dishpan, full at last, is put on the drainboard. Starting to scrub a skillet, I quote from a poem in yesterday's English lesson: " '*Work—work—work! / From weary chime to chime, / Work—work—work, / As prisoners work for crime!*' "

Dad laughs. "Yes, you're really put upon! One job a day to do, and you groan!"

" '*Work—work—work! My labor never flags; / And what are its wages? A bed of straw, / A crust of bread—and rags.*' "

Dad laughs again. "There's a child-labor law. Maybe you ought to report me to the authorities!"

"Maybe I will! Meanwhile, you can dry this." I hand him the skillet. "But, you know, we could have a double sink here."

He nods. "Yes, but it would be expensive to install. These cabinets would have to be knocked out and new ones built, and the plumbing would be a problem. When a house gets to be as old as this one, you can't do one thing but what two or three more are necessary. The whole place is needing so much done to it that it really might be sensible to think about a new one."

A pot slips from my hand and soapy water is sloshed onto the floor. Dad finds the mop and makes a couple of swipes with it. The suds on the floor remind me of the time Mom let the sink overflow. She had left water running while she answered the telephone. The conversation had lasted till she noticed soapsuds, in a trickle of water, coming toward her, two rooms away. Daisy and Irene had been spending the night away from home, and I had helped mop up the water. Mom and I were drying the floor when Dad got home, and Mom had said, "Sometimes things happen that we don't really plan." Dad had offered to take us out to eat so she wouldn't have to work in a wet kitchen, and we had ridden up Highway 41 to a barbecue place near the overhead bridge. Mom had said it was so nice to eat out that she must flood the house again sometime.

Dad continues: "Of course, if we buy a new house we'll sell this place, but it's the land here that's valuable. Whoever buys it will probably tear down the house first thing."

"Good!" says Daisy. "I hate this old house."

"I don't," says Dad. "I've lived in it all my life, and it's important to me. But your mother would probably agree with you. She never has taken to this house, maybe because at first we more or less had to live in it."

"Why?" asks Daisy.

"Well, until recently it was all we could afford. Also, my mother needed us here with her."

I cannot remember Granny Ponder, but I have heard that she was a difficult old lady. When my parents got married, my father brought Mom home to help look after the household, which included his mother and uncle. Uncle Roy was an invalid, mentally off balance as well as physically weak, and he became such a problem after the death of Granny that eventually he was taken to a nursing home. He is dead now, but I can remember him. He would shout at Mom to do this and do that, never being satisfied with anything she did—always telling her to do something else. She never lost patience with him.

Dad tells Daisy, "Your mother always wanted me to build a house, or buy a new one—'one without ghosts,' she used to say. Maybe if we buy a house now she'll hurry home. Maybe she'll decide we need her more than the Rockdales." Dad never refers to his cousin Tom only. He sounds as if Mom is helping all the relatives in Montgomery. "Wouldn't it be interesting," he says, "if having a filling station next door turns out to be lucky for us? Our lot would be a good one for some commercial outfit, and I might even throw in the three and a half acres back of us. Altogether the place should bring a fine price."

"If you made lots of money on it," says Daisy, "maybe Alice Evans and the others will quit saying you aren't very shrewd in business and that you let ol' Doc Swanson cheat you."

"Is that what they're saying? Well, you can tell 'em they're wrong. I sold Doc Swanson the lot next door, and while I did sell it to him because he said he wanted to build a house on it, I sold it to him with no stipulations. I was not cheated."

I speak up: "You were not cheated outright. But you know and I know and everybody else knows that ol' Doc bought the lot from you, pretending he wanted to live on it, and then turned around and sold it for a big profit to the oil company."

"He says he didn't know the oil company wanted it till later. And the offer was 'too attractive,' in his words, to turn down."

I laugh. "And you believe him?"

"I trust people. Unless I know for a hard-down fact a reason not to, I trust people."

"That's what Grady Maxwell said," says Daisy. "He said

you trusted people too much. He heard his mother saying it on account of Mom being away so long."

"Well, maybe she'll come home if we get us a new house. In the meantime don't let what anyone says bother you."

"Leona Hawkins says that we're washed-out southern gentility," says Daisy, catching her breath to explain: "Gentility means refined and just real, real elegant." She smiles as if we have been complimented.

I say, "And washed-out means we ain't got it anymore," and her smile vanishes.

Dad asks, "Where would Leona have gotten any such notion?"

"From her sister, Martha. She's been to New York and seen plays and things, and she's studied drama in college besides, and she says there's a playwright . . ."

She pauses to explain the word, but Dad teases her: "I suppose you expect us to believe that a playwright is someone who writes plays!"

"Yes, and there's one that has written plays about southerners whose families used to be something but are not so special now. And Leona asked Martha if anybody in Ellenville is like that, and Martha said that she supposed we came as close to it as anybody, us living over here in this old house that's falling to pieces while folks who were our grandfather's hired hands are buying modern residences."

She pauses, but I beat her to the explanation. "We know! Residences are where people live, modern or otherwise."

"Well, anyway, I think it's all very edifying."

"Edifying as can be!" I say.

Dad laughs. "And maybe true to a point. My parents had some money—not much—and a little land. The generation before them had more, but it was divided so many ways that by the time my turn came, there was no money left to inherit. But I did get a little of the land. For years it wasn't worth anything, and I sold some of it for almost nothing. But prices are up nowadays."

I say, "With Atlanta so near, and new highways being built, one of these days we'll be a suburb of the city."

"Your mother thinks I should have been able to see ahead and that I should have held on to more of the land till prices went higher."

"Nobody can see ahead," I say, angrily. I wish Dad had sounded mad too. I wish his temper would flare up sometimes. "Mom ought to have known that you had no way of seeing into the future."

"Yes," he agrees. "But sometimes women think we men should have done better." Once I had heard Mom telling Dad that he should be more aggressive. She had said that other men in his position would have found a way to buy an appliance store and run it for themselves instead of operating it for someone else. She had been wanting him to ask for a raise, but he had insisted that he was paid as high a salary as the business could afford. "Anyway," he had added, "we have everything we need." Mom had answered, "You have everything *you* need."

"She thinks I haven't managed too well," says Dad, "but maybe I'll begin to do better." He looks as if he's thinking about what he could have done to make things different. Then he smiles. "Maybe I'll learn to be shrewd! Maybe I'll get us a whopping, fat amount for this place if we decide to let it go."

"Let's do let it go," urges Daisy. "Let's sell it and buy a brand-new house in a brand-new neighborhood."

"And a brand-new mother!" I say. "Maybe if you get a high enough price for this place you can get a new house and a new wife."

"Don't say that!" scolds Dad. "Sometimes your tongue is too sharp, Alan, and you say things you don't mean!"

"But I do mean it. Why don't you get a divorce? Then you'd be free to marry again if you wanted to."

"But I love your mother, and we're married to each other. That's why."

"If she loved you she'd come home."

"She'll come home."

I look at him. "I hope not. I hope she never comes back."

The Plan

"Hap said to invite you and Amanda to go with us to the movie Friday night," says Irene. She has just come in from a date, and we are in the upstairs room. Daisy and Dad have gone to bed, and I have been reading. Irene has been out with Hap Jordan. He's the only child of the richest family in Ellenville, and my friends and I consider him a playboy. He has gone with first one girl and then another, dating each one a few weeks or months and then breaking up, but he and Irene have been together for more than a year. It is something of a record.

"I don't know if I have enough money for Friday night," I say. "But maybe I can hit Dad for a few extra dollars." Last summer I clerked in Colby's, the hardware store, and I work there now on Saturdays, but I'm never ahead on cash.

"Oh, don't worry about finances. Hap'll pay. He's generous with his money, and his folks give him so much it keeps him busy finding ways to spend it."

I laugh. "Well, let him spend it on you! He could buy you expensive presents."

"I'll bet some people do think I'm going with Hap for his money."

"You wouldn't be the first girl who had."

"Maybe that's what he likes about me. I'm not impressed that he's rich." She lowers her voice to confide in me: "I refused to accept a Christmas gift he brought me."

"But you got a gift from him: the manicure set. Don't you remember?"

"He brought it along as a 'small extra.' My real present was a watch set in diamonds."

"Why didn't you keep it?"

"I didn't think it was appropriate for him to give it to me, that's why." She adjusts the watch on her wrist. "Noble of me, wasn't it, considering this one is on its last lap."

"Dad and Daisy and I might give you a new one for graduation. Or will Hap bring back the Christmas one for graduation?"

"No, I've just told you that I don't want expensive presents from him." She smiles. "Of course, he has so much more than money."

"Like what?"

"Like good looks—and real charm. Why, he's so persuasive—fresh at times!—that it's not easy to resist him. And he has a good mind. He doesn't always use it, but it's there! Would you believe that he's leading the class in some of his subjects?"

"He ought to be leading it in every subject! He's had all of them before." Hap failed to graduate last year. Being an athletic hero, star of the football and basketball teams, with letters in track and baseball—besides girl chasing—he had not found time to study. Because he was on the varsity four years, this year he has not been allowed to participate in sports. It's given him time to discover the classroom. "I'd guess you've been a good influence on him," I say. "And I'll have to admit Hap's okay. He never has tried to push the rest of us around the way your old pal David used to do."

"Well, what do you want me to tell him?"

"Tell him I said he's an improvement over David!"

"Oh, you know what I mean: about the movie. It was his idea. When he asked if I'd like to see *Gone with the Wind* while it's back in Atlanta, I mentioned that you and Amanda had been wanting Dad to take you, and Hap said, 'Well, let's invite 'em to go with us.' "

"I'll check with Amanda tomorrow," I say, starting to my room. "But she's been sort of moody lately. Something's bothering her."

After roll call I tell Amanda about the invitation. "I don't know if I can go," she says just as the bell rings for classes.

At lunch we are with the crowd, and it is after school before we are by ourselves again. "Will you walk home with me?" she asks.

"Sure, but aren't we stopping by the house?"

"No, Mamma has decided that you and I are not to study together in the afternoons or see each other except at school. You were in on the beginning of it."

"I thought maybe she would ease up."

"So did I, but she won't. I can't even stop off at the drugstore with you. In fact, you'll have to turn back before we round the corner near my house."

I say bitterly, "The Ponders are not 'the right people' anymore!"

"You know how Mamma is."

"I know how she was about Grady," I say. Two years ago when Amanda's sister, Ellie, had been dating Grady Fulton, Mrs. Moore had decided that he lacked what she considered "background" and had insisted that Ellie give him up. At first Ellie and Grady grew closer together than ever; they had written notes to each other and met secretly. Amanda and I had been parties to the conspiracy. Eventually Ellie had decided that her mother was right—social position mattered—but not until she had another boyfriend.

"She made Ellie give up Grady, and now she's making you give me up," I say as we get to the corner. We stand facing each other. I am mad at Mrs. Moore, but I take out my anger on Amanda. Staring at her angrily, I add, "Or maybe you want to give me up?"

"Maybe I do." She stares back at me. Then she laughs as if she has been teasing.

She hurries away, and I go to the drugstore, where I drink a milk shake with Lanky and Blake. I nod at Hap and Irene, who are parked in front, as I am leaving. Hap calls, "Are you and Amanda going with us Friday night?"

"We'd like to," I answer, going over to his car. "We thank you for the invitation, but Amanda's not certain her mother will let her go. In fact, she's almost certain she won't."

"Why not? Your own sister will be along. What sort of trouble does Mrs. Moore think Amanda'll get into with a setup like that?"

"Well, to tell you the truth, she's wanting Amanda and me to quit seeing each other. Our family is not considered respectable now."

"Aw, hell!" says Hap. Then he asks, "Do you suppose Mrs. Moore would let Amanda have a date with me?"

"Now wait a minute!" says Irene, as I answer the question: "She probably would. You're respectable."

"For all Mrs. Moore knows, at any rate!" says Hap. To Irene he explains, "I could pick up Amanda Friday on my way to your house; then we could all go to the movie together." He looks at me. "Tell Amanda the plan, and I'll call her tomorrow afternoon. If Mrs. Moore answers I'll tell her I'm wondering whether I'd be permitted to invite Amanda to go with me to see *Gone with the Wind*. You'll be surprised at how it'll work out!"

The next day I tell Amanda, and after school Hap and Irene stop at our house for him to make the call. Amanda answers, and Hap says, "You heard the plan, didn't you? If your mother is listening, pretend I'm asking you for a date and say whatever you think will please her. I'm turning the phone over to Alan."

"I'm here," I say, and Amanda begins, "Well, Hap Jordan, this is a surprise!" sounding as if it is. She begins a monologue, making it sound like one end of a conversation: "Well, I don't know. . . . Yes, I have more or less broken up with Alan, not that we were ever anything more than childhood pals. But I thought you were going steady with Irene. . . ." She pauses as if an explanation is being offered.

"You're doing great," I say.

"Well, yes, I'd like to. Sure, I'd like to a lot, but it's just that I don't know if Mamma, that is, my parents, will let me. But since it's for Friday, and . . . What's that? . . . Yes, I've been wanting to see it. I saw it two years ago when it first came out—Mr. and Mrs. Ponder took Alan and me—but I want to see it again. If you'll just stop talking, I'll go and ask her."

She puts the phone down, and I hear her saying, "Hap

Jordan wants to know if I can go to Atlanta to see *Gone with the Wind.*"

"I thought he dated Irene Ponder," says her mother. I can hear the conversation clearly.

"Well, he did. But he's dated lots of girls, you know that. You used to say you wished he would pay some attention to Ellie."

"Why did he say he wasn't going with Irene?"

Amanda laughs. "So you heard me asking him! Well, he didn't give me a satisfactory answer, not really. He mumbled something about variety being important to a growing boy, but you know as well as I do what's behind it. His parents have probably laid down the law at his house too. But may I go?"

"Isn't he a good bit older than you?"

"He's a senior," says Amanda, not saying that this is the second year he's been a senior. "And I'd be too if I hadn't lost a year."

"I suppose it's all right," says Mrs. Moore. "We'll have to clear it with your father, but go ahead and accept. I'm sure it will be all right." I'm sure of it too. And I'm sure that Amanda wishes there were a chance that her father would ever disagree with Mrs. Moore about anything.

Amanda picks up the phone. "Hap? Hap, are you there?"

"You're a good actress," I say, "and an even better liar!"

"Oh, there you are!" says Amanda. "No. No, she didn't say I couldn't go. Yes, that's right. . . . Fine. . . . Quarter till seven, I'll be ready." And she hangs up the telephone.

"My mother's so excited," she tells me the next day. "You'd think *she* had a date with Hap Jordan!"

"I enjoyed your performance while I was on the phone."

"I put on a better one afterwards, and I've never seen Mamma so happy. She left off polishing the candelabra to tell me what I must do. 'Wear your powder-blue dress,' she said. 'It's sweet.' " Amanda makes a face. "But I may wear it, anyway, since the joke is on her. She'll think I'm dressing up to please Hap. I even went into Ellie's room to borrow makeup and stuff from her dresser."

Amanda used to say that Ellie primped all the time. Ellie is not as naturally pretty as Amanda, but she has always taken more pains with her looks. Their aunt from Santa Fe, New Mexico, visits the Moores every summer, and she had labeled them Ellie, the Beauty, and Amanda, the Brain. Amanda had not liked being called the Brain, although she didn't mind that Ellie was considered the Beauty. When she had told me about it, I had helped her think of other names for herself. We had fun one afternoon making them up, settling on Amanda, the Gioconda, as our favorite. We had read that *La Gioconda* is another name for Mona Lisa, the painting, and the sound of it coupled with *Amanda* appealed to us. For the rest of the afternoon Amanda had tried smiling like Mona Lisa, having me tell her when I felt she was doing it right. I think of this when she tells me about going into Ellie's room to gather up powder and paint. "Amanda, the Gioconda, is to turn into Amanda, the Beauty," I tell her.

"No such thing," she says. "But I do have an appointment after school tomorrow with Mrs. Dalton." Mrs. Dalton does the hair of Gloria Mason and some of the other girls who go to a beauty parlor. Such things have never been of interest to Amanda, and I say so.

"It's all a joke," she replies. "A great big joke!"

"Did your mother insist that you make the appointment?"

"No, I thought of it myself."

I mean to tease her when I ask, "Is it you or your mother who's excited about the date with Hap?"

Amanda looks startled. Then she says softly, "What if the joke's on me?"

Gone with the Wind

The day we are to go to the movie I stay after school and toss a baseball back and forth with Blake Rhodes. He hopes to be Ellenville's star pitcher. Coach Wilkins asks me if I won't try out for the team, but I cannot. I had corrective surgery on one of my legs in the fall, and if I am careful for another couple of months the doctors assure me there'll be no more trouble. "Next year I'll try out for everything," I tell Coach.

"Good!" he says. "I'll need you."

Because it is Friday some of our friends have left early, but Blake and I stay until the coach calls time on us. We shower quickly, and I hurry home and am eating a sandwich when the doorbell rings. "I'll get it," yells Daisy, who has never missed answering the bell when Irene is expecting a date.

Irene calls from upstairs, "Tell him I'll be right there."

I finish a glass of iced tea and go into the front hall.

Hap, in the living room with Daisy, motions to me that Amanda is in the car.

She is sitting in the front seat, and I lift a hand in greeting as I start to get into the back. Amanda gets out, and I realize too late that I should have held the door open—or at least waited for her. "I don't really have a date with Hap," she says. "Did you think I was going to sit beside him on the way to Atlanta?"

I return to the sidewalk. "I'm sorry," I say, and I am sorry. "I wasn't thinking." Then I look at her, and I think for a moment that I am imagining what I see. The hairstyle makes the biggest difference. It's the way Deanna Durbin wore hers in *Nice Girl,* the last movie we saw. It makes Amanda look as if she too has suddenly quit being a child star and is ready to take on the role of a young woman. Also, she's done something to her eyebrows, and she's using makeup. Her shoes are high-heeled, and her dress is the prettiest blue I've ever seen. I am stunned by the transformation and should tell her how great she looks, but instead I mumble, "I'd forgotten this was a big deal." It disappoints her, I'm sure, but she laughs. I add, "You look different."

"You don't," she says, and I know what she means. I have on the same dark-green sweater that I wore to school today, and a pair of slacks that would look better if they were pressed. "You look fine just the way you are," she says. "If you ever get dressed up, somebody'll take you away from me."

I say, "You're dressed up—" but Irene interrupts me. She and Hap have come out to the car. "Are you two going with us?" she asks. "Or are you going to stand on the sidewalk till we get back?"

Quickly I open the back door and Amanda gets into the car. She is settling just inside until she realizes that I am crawling in beside her. I should have gone around to the opposite door, but it is too late now. Amanda makes room for me.

Instead of sliding all the way across the seat, she stops just beyond the middle. As we start off she looks up, and Hap sees her in the rear-view mirror. He winks, and Amanda moves nearer the window, away from me.

After the movie we stop at the Varsity, near the Georgia Tech campus, and order hot dogs and orange drinks, specialties of the drive-in. While waiting we talk about the movie and how we live in the area where much of the story took place. Irene says, "Wouldn't it have been fun to go to a barbecue where everybody came on fine horses or in wagons and buggies!"

"What if it rained?" asks Hap.

"Pessimist!" she says. "It wouldn't rain on the day of the barbecue!"

"All right, count me in!" He says he'd like to have lived in Civil War days and been Rhett Butler.

"I'd like to have worn the fashions of those days," says Irene. "Can you imagine how many yards of material some of those dresses took?" Then she adds, "But wasn't Scarlett terrible, really? She was selfish and calculating."

"She was strong," says Amanda, as if being strong cancels out less attractive qualities. "And she knew what she wanted."

"Why, she didn't," I say. "She wanted one thing till she got it, and then she wanted something else. Anyway, I don't like anything about those times. I'd rather be alive today." I raise my voice. "The South is still recuperating from the mess we got into then. The rest of you can put your hands over your hearts and talk about 'our glorious past' all you want to, but not me." I sound as if I am mad with everyone in the car.

"I didn't say it was all that glorious," protests Amanda.

"Neither did I," says Hap. "But I still would like to have been a blockade runner."

I don't know what's the matter with me, but I realize it's not the discussion of the Civil War that is making me irritable. Although I know that I am being disagreeable, I continue: "People always think that if they'd been alive in those days they'd have been the dashing hero or the belle of the barbecue. But somebody had to fight the war, and everybody suffered in the end."

"Go away!" says Irene. "You're letting a little thing like history interfere with our dreams of grandeur. You know too many facts."

"Maybe so," I agree, sorry for my outburst.

Irene tells Hap, "That's the trouble with him. He's cram full of facts!"

"I'd rather be full of hot dogs," says Hap. "I wish our order would come on. It's getting late."

"Dad won't be worried about me since Alan's along," says Irene. "What about you, Amanda?"

"After the way Hap dazzled my mother when he came for me, she wouldn't worry if I stayed out all night!" Hap and Irene laugh, but it is not funny to me. I hate Mrs. Moore for accepting Hap and turning me away.

Irene asks Hap, "What'd you do?" and Amanda answers for him. "He asked Mamma if she wouldn't like to just come on and go to the movie with us! What would you have done, Hap, if she'd said, 'Why, yes, you darling boy, I believe I will'?"

"I'm not sure. I guess I'd have had some explaining to do when we picked up Irene and Alan."

"You could have told her Irene and I had a date with each other," I say angrily. "She's convinced that we're decadent, anyway." There is a moment when no one says anything. Then our order arrives, and we concentrate on food.

As we leave the parking lot, Hap says, "Alan, if you were big enough to drive you could chauffeur us home."

Several of my friends, with birthdays ahead of mine, have their driver's license already, but I must wait until June. I correct Hap: "I'm big enough; I'm just not old enough."

"*I'm* old enough," says Amanda.

"Do you have your license?" he asks.

"Yes, I passed the test. But I haven't driven very much. Dad's always too busy to help me."

"I'll help you sometime," says Hap. "Any time you want a lesson, I'll give it to you."

Amanda thanks him, and soon Irene and Hap are in a conversation with each other. He puts his arm around her shoulder, pulling her nearer to him. She moves closer, but when he leans over and kisses her she tells him to keep his eyes on the road.

I put my arm around Amanda, and she slides nearer to me. We sit for a long time without speaking. In all the years we have been together it is the first time that neither of us has anything to say. She seems almost a stranger to me—an exciting, new person. I want us to kiss, to be close together the way we were on the afternoon Dad called us downstairs. I want to put both arms around her, and I think how good it would be to lie with her on the back seat. I remind myself that we are not alone, and I take my arm from around her shoulder.

"You don't have to keep your eyes on the road," she whispers.

"Yes, I do. I have to watch where we're going."

After a while we arrive home. Hap and Irene get out, lingering at the corner of the house that is shaded from the streetlight. Amanda and I stay in the car. "You might say this is our first real date," says Amanda.

"You might," I agree. I put one arm around her, and we are quiet again. Then I say, "We're supposed to kiss good night." It sounds stupid, and Amanda laughs.

"There's no law that we must!" she says as I press my lips to hers. Her arms go over my shoulders, but not with the same urgency of the afternoon we were upstairs.

I push my other arm back of her, around her waist, and we are half sitting, half lying when Hap opens the door. It usually takes him longer to say good night to Irene; I've often heard them whispering to each other. It worries me that he is in a hurry tonight.

"Ponders out!" he says, and I sit up.

"I could ride over to the Moores with you and walk back," I suggest.

"Better not. As far as Mrs. Moore knows, Amanda and I have been to Atlanta by ourselves."

I half stumble from the car. Amanda follows me, and I'm surprised. "Oh, you're getting up front?"

"Now really!" she says in a tone adults use in talking to children. "If Mamma happened to see us drive up, don't you think she'd wonder why I was in the back seat alone?" At that, she and Hap laugh as if it's the funniest thing they've ever heard.

A strange sensation comes over me as I watch them drive away. It is a gnawing, unpleasant feeling—jealousy. I should be seeing Amanda home. I wish I had not been a part of tonight's plan.

In the kitchen Irene is raiding the refrigerator. "I shouldn't be hungry," she says, "but I am." She pours herself a glass of milk and glances at me. "I've never seen Amanda looking so good." I say nothing, and she continues: "Why, she's turned into a rare beauty."

"She's always been a rare beauty," I say.

"Yes, but all of a sudden she sparkles."

"She got all prettied up so Mrs. Moore would think she was excited about having a date with Hap." I almost snarl when I say it.

"He was doing you a favor," says Irene, kicking a shoe into the air. It lands in the corner. "Maybe he'll take you and Amanda with us again; I thought it was fun."

"I wonder what Mrs. Moore'll think if she sees you and Hap out somewhere? Amanda told her you'd broken up."

"Well, she can always tell her we went back together."

I shrug. "I guess that'd explain why Hap doesn't call Amanda for another date."

Irene has finished drinking the milk. After rinsing the glass, she starts to her room. "Who knows?" she says nonchalantly. "Maybe he'll call her again."

Message from Buddy

Saturdays I work at Colby's, the biggest hardware store in Ellenville. Stock ranges from plowshares to expensive dishes. It is almost time for spring planting, and my customers this morning are farmers. I measure rope and locate parts for cultivators and harrows without thinking. My mind is on last night. I make a mistake in ringing up a sale and do not catch it. The customer does. Loudly. He accuses me of trying to cheat him out of forty-seven cents. Mr. Colby comes over to see what's wrong. The man complains to him, "You ought not to let kids run your store."

"Alan's the only clerk I have who's under twenty-one," says Mr. Colby, "and I apologize for the mistake."

"I'm sorry too," I tell the man, handing him his money.

He walks away, and Mr. Colby tells me, "Don't let it happen again!" I put last night out of my mind and concentrate on business.

At home for lunch I try to call Amanda, although I don't

know what I plan to say. I must not ask, "Did you and Hap go straight home after you left our house?"

Mrs. Moore answers the telephone and tells me that Amanda is out. When I ask where, she says, "It's really not your concern, but she's at the library."

I stop at the library on my way back to Colby's. Amanda isn't there, and when I call her home on Saturday night Mrs. Moore tells me that she's out. She does not say where. Sunday afternoon I try again. "Yes," says Mrs. Moore, "Amanda's here, but I think it would be best if you don't call her again—ever." I wait, holding the telephone to my ear in disbelief. After a moment there is a click at the other end of the line as Mrs. Moore hangs up.

In the upstairs room Irene and Daisy are listening to the radio. Their favorite Sunday-afternoon program, "Swing and Sway with Sammy Kaye," is on. I am not in the mood for it, so I go to my room and begin tomorrow's English assignment. Mrs. Hatcher asked us to read poetry for pleasure over the weekend, finding selections that are not in our literature book. "And bring a poem to share with the class," she had said. "Bring one that speaks to you personally."

I doubt that a poem can get through to me now, but I will see. I read the index of one book after another, but nothing attracts me. Nothing "speaks to me personally," and it occurs to me that I am not likely to come across a poem entitled "Go to Hell, Mrs. Moore." The idea of such an offering makes me feel better, and remembering the first part of the assignment I start reading for pleasure. Gradually I lose myself in the effort, and in late afternoon I decide that "you shall above all things be glad and young," by e e cummings, will be mine for tomorrow.

Monday morning I am back to being indignant because Mrs. Moore would not let me speak to Amanda. I expect Amanda to be angry too, but she says only, "I was in my room when you called, reading poetry for pleasure. Mrs. Hatcher asked us to, remember?"

"Nobody asked us to refuse to take telephone calls."

"I didn't refuse to take one."

"But you're not mad that your mother wouldn't call you."

"No, I'm not mad," she says. "You're the one who's mad. What did you want? You can tell me now."

"I didn't want anything," I say angrily, and she laughs, which infuriates me.

I sulk throughout the day. By last period I am still not in a good humor when Mrs. Hatcher asks us to share our findings of the weekend. "Rick, we'll start with you," she says. She usually calls on him first, maybe wanting to get his answers out of the way.

Rick says, "Well, I believe I like . . . let me think, oh, yes, 'O Captain! My Captain!' best."

"You seem to have forgotten that you were to bring in a poem *not* in our text. But never mind, you may stick with your choice if you'll tell me why it appeals to you."

"Oh, I didn't know that was part of the assignment," says Rick.

Mrs. Hatcher puts a mark in her roll book and calls on Gloria Mason, who is sitting next to me. As usual, she is busy writing a note, but she hears Mrs. Hatcher call on her. "I'm sorry, Mrs. Hatcher, but my Uncle Carl died, and we went to Jacksonville for the funeral and didn't get back till late last night."

"I'll give you a zero," says Mrs. Hatcher, "but if you'll

bring in a poem later I'll change it." Then she asks Amanda if she found a poem that appealed to her.

"Yes, ma'am," answers Amanda. "It's 'New Love and Old,' by Sara Teasdale." She reads it: " '*In my heart the old love / Struggled with the new; / It was ghostly waking / All night through. / Dear things, kind things, / That my old love said, / Ranged themselves reproachfully / Round my bed.*' "

She's gone stark, raving crazy, I tell myself. She doesn't like that kind of poetry. "*Dear things, kind things*"! That's not like her.

" '*But I could not heed them,*' " she continues, " '*For I seemed to see / The eyes of my new love / Fixed on me. / Old love, old love, / How can I be true? / Shall I be faithless to myself / Or to you?*' "

She is telling me something. It is our old way of talking to each other through the lines of a poet. I brood about it instead of listening to what Mrs. Hatcher says about the selection. I do not hear what anyone else reads to the class, but toward the end of the period I hear my name called. I do not answer. Mrs. Hatcher says again, "Alan, it's your turn."

The cummings book is on top of my desk, a scrap of paper marking the title of the poem that I had planned to read. But I no longer believe what it says: "you shall above all things be glad and young." It's not all that good to be young, and I'm not glad about anything. "I don't have a poem," I say and Mrs. Hatcher puts a mark in her book. It is the only zero I have ever received, but there has to be a first time for everything. I look down, scowling, and for the rest of the period I study Gloria Mason's legs.

After the final bell I ask Amanda about her poem.

"Oh," she says as we're leaving the building, "I just had to have something for the assignment, so I brought it along." She holds up the book, *The Collected Poems of Sara Teasdale*.

I say disgustedly, "To have spent all weekend looking, it seems to me you could have found something better than that." I turn and start toward the sidewalk, but she does not follow me. "Aren't you coming?" I had taken it for granted that I would walk her to the corner near her house.

"No, I'm catching a ride with Karen Allison from now on." Karen is a senior who drives her mother's car to school.

At home I make myself a peanut butter and fig preserve sandwich and then settle into the upstairs room to listen to records. Just after I get there Daisy comes in from the drugstore, rattling ice in a paper cup. "You've got to help me with my geography," she says.

"I haven't got to do anything."

"Daddy said you did. He said so last night."

"He said maybe I'd help you."

"All right," she says, heading toward the door. "If I fail it'll be your fault."

"Bring the book," I order, and soon we are busy. I call out states and wait for her to name the capitals.

A cardinal lights on a branch of the holly tree, and Daisy says, "Look! A message from Buddy!"

"What is it?" I ask.

"You can make it up."

"I'm busy with your geography lesson whether you are or not."

"Well," says Daisy, pausing a moment, "Buddy said to tell you that Hap and Amanda are in love."

"What?" I shout, slamming the book shut and throwing

it onto the table. "Where'd you get an idea like that?"

"It wasn't me who sent the message," she says. "It was Buddy."

The fifth amendment, I realize, and of course I know the rules. "Well, I wonder how Buddy got such a crack-brained notion." I try not to sound annoyed. I have used the fifth amendment more than once to get a rise out of somebody else. It works against me now.

"I heard it at school today," says Daisy, volunteering more information than the rules require.

"When I'm grown," I say, "I'll live in a city so big that nobody'll know anybody else's business. This whole town knows everything everybody does by the time they do it."

"Does everybody know Hap and Amanda are in love?"

"Oh, don't be such a bat-brain! Somebody probably saw Hap picking her up the other night. It doesn't take much to get a rumor started around here, and anyway, Hap and Irene are out together right now. He's bringing her home from school, same as always."

"I know, I saw them at the drugstore a while ago. But Amanda's not here—the same as always!"

"She's not here because her mother has put a stop to her being here."

Daisy looks at me, smirking, as if she knows everything there is to know and that it's too bad I'm so naive. "Her mother could never make Amanda do anything she doesn't want to do." I know this is so, and it makes me mad. "And, anyway, why would Mrs. Moore just suddenly decide not to let Amanda come here?"

I stare at her angrily. "She says she does not want Amanda to have anything else to do with us because we might contaminate her."

"Why?"

"Because our mother is a slut."

Daisy's expression changes. Her smirk disappears, and she turns pale. I am afraid she will faint. It is bad enough for her classmates to remind her that things have gone wrong; she should not have to hear it at home. Besides, I made up what Mrs. Moore had said. But I'm right, I say to myself, that's exactly what Mrs. Moore meant, and I get madder. I am furious with Amanda and her mother, with my mother, with Daisy—and with myself for hurting my sister.

Daisy starts from the room. "I've studied enough," she says, her voice trembling.

I should follow her and apologize. I should do something to make her feel better. I could offer to help Irene with supper tonight. That would give Daisy a chance to listen to "Scattergood Baines" and "Sidewalk Snoopers." She's always complaining that her friends get to listen to them, but that she has to work while they're on. She's saving her money to buy a radio for the kitchen. Meanwhile, I should ask her to forgive me, but I do not make a move, not even to put more records on the player. As far as I'm concerned, the last one can play forever.

10
Two Apart

Last Friday at this time I was gulping down supper before starting to Atlanta. Tonight there is no hurry; I am not going anywhere.

The telephone rings, and Irene leaves the table to answer it. Dad continues to talk about a house that Mr. Larrick, the contractor, has almost finished.

"Let's buy it," says Daisy. "Let's do."

"It's the right size for us," says Dad. "And a realty company from Atlanta has made me a firm offer on this house. They want the lot for a client of theirs—a food chain, I believe."

"Goody!" says Daisy.

"But all of you will have to agree that we're willing to give up this ol' place. I don't want to sell and then everybody start crying, 'This is home! We don't want to leave!' "

"Well, I vote for moving," says Daisy.

I do not act as if it matters to me one way or the other,

but of course it does. I cannot imagine living anywhere except in this house. I wonder if Mom would come back if we had a new one. The main arguments between her and Dad that I've ever known about had to do with the house. He liked it the way it was; she wanted it remodeled if he would not buy a new one. I had agreed with her, but I would not want to agree with her about anything now. I wonder too if Amanda's mother might approve of us if we had a new home. Maybe she would be impressed, but it is too late for her opinion to make any difference. Dad and Daisy are still talking. "Well, I vote for moving," says Daisy again.

"Me too," I say.

"Then we'll wait and see how Irene feels," says Dad.

"It doesn't matter how she votes," argues Daisy. "Alan and I are for it, and that's a majority." She catches her breath and explains: "That's when you get the most votes."

"Is that a fact?" teases Dad.

"And it's a very democratic way to do things," continues Daisy. "Two out of three of us means sixty-six and two-thirds percent, and that's way over half. So it really doesn't matter about Irene. She's only thirty-three and one-third percent, and that's a minority."

She catches her breath, but I speak first: "And that means you've read another chapter in your civics book and you know some arithmetic. Bright kid!"

"Don't aggravate your sister," says Dad. Then he turns to Daisy. "But Irene's vote does matter. The decision must be unanimous." Smiling, he adds, "That's when you get *all* the votes."

Irene comes back into the dining room looking dazed, as if someone has knocked the senses out of her. She sits down but gets up immediately and starts toward the kitchen. A moment later she returns with a freezer tray of ice cream. "Here's our dessert," she says, putting aside one of the four bowls at the end of the table. "I don't care for any, but I'll dip some for the rest of you."

"You've got to vote first," says Daisy. "Would you be willing for Dad to sell this old house and buy that new one across town?"

"I'd be willing for Dad to decide."

"But he wants to be sure that none of us minds giving up this house."

"I don't mind," says Irene.

"You can leave the ice cream," says Dad, "and Daisy'll dip it for us. Go ahead and get ready for your date."

"I don't have a date. It's been broken."

"I'll bet Hap's got a date with Amanda," says Daisy. "Is that what the call was about?"

"Dip the ice cream," I say irritably. "And mind your own business!"

Monday I arrive at school late—but not late enough. I had hoped homeroom period would be over. Mrs. Rogers is in the office and everyone is chatting noisily. There's a lull as I settle into the desk next to Amanda's. I go to the corner and sharpen pencils, hoping the bell will ring by the time I return to my desk. When it doesn't, I get out a book and flip through it.

The room quiets down as if everyone wants to hear what Amanda and I will say to each other. Finally Amanda closes her notebook and turns to me. "I guess you've heard," she whispers.

"Heard what?" I ask, louder than I mean to, and the room suddenly is completely silent. Amanda opens her notebook again. When a few people go back to chatting, she turns to me again. "That Hap and I are going together."

"I've heard," I say, softer this time. I do not say anything else, and neither does she. Nor do we pretend to study. Both of us sit with our hands folded, staring straight ahead, until the bell rings.

None of our morning classes are together, and often we do not see each other after homeroom until midday. Occasionally we have met in the hall between second and third period when I'm heading for geometry and she's going to French. Today I take a longer route in order to avoid a chance meeting. We meet in the hall; Amanda has taken the same route. "Oh, hi," she says, and I nod.

"Let's talk at lunchtime," she says.

I walk down the hall as if I have not heard.

All year she and I have eaten lunch together. I have study hall just before noon, and she has economics. Always I have lagged behind when my group starts down the chow line, and she catches up with me. Today I am first in line from study hall instead of waiting for her, but we meet as we are leaving the lunchroom. She whispers, "If you don't want to hear what I've got to say, I can't make you listen."

"I don't want to hear," I say angrily.

"I didn't want to hurt you," she says as I start away. I hope that she is following me, that she will make me listen. I am behaving childishly and I know it; I do not understand myself or her. All I know is that I am hurt and I am mad. She does not follow me, and I go early to chemistry lab, wishing I knew what to combine that would blow the school—and myself and Amanda—to bits.

At the beginning of last period I meet Roy Nelson as I

start into English. "Say, Roy, what about trading places with me this period?"

"Sure, why not?" He understands. But inside we find that Amanda has traded places and is sitting near Roy's desk. "The joke's on us!" says Roy, going to his usual place as I sit down at mine. Amanda has swapped places with Nettie Veal, a good student. I know that Amanda has not put her back here because she wants someone bright near me; she chose her because she's homely. I greet Nettie and then turn to Gloria Mason, sitting on the other side of me.

"Help me with the lesson, quick!" she pleads. "I forgot to open the book."

I am about to ask if that's anything new, but her smile is so nice that I hate to make it disappear. And when I glance at Amanda and see that she is glancing at me, I lean over to Gloria. "Why, sure! I'll be glad to help you." As if I don't have a book of my own, I lean closer and flip through the pages of her literature text, placing one arm casually on the back of her chair. "Actually, we're mostly going to review," I tell her. Then an idea comes to me. "But, say, did you ever bring in a poem that speaks to you personally?"

"Oh, you're right!" she says, "and my grades don't need that zero. But if this is the last day on poetry—"

I interrupt her. "I know just the poem for you," I say, getting out *The Collected Poems of Sara Teasdale.* I borrowed the book from the town library after Amanda returned it. "Look at this one." I open the book to page thirty. "It speaks to you so personally that Mrs. Hatcher is bound to give you an A plus."

Gloria reads the poem and giggles. "Why, Alan, it says just exactly the way I feel every time I have a new boyfriend!"

Mrs. Hatcher comes in and sits on the edge of the table in front of us. After calling the roll she says, "I'm sure all of you know this is our last day on poetry. So we'll talk about anything having to do with it that interests you."

Gloria raises her hand and asks, "Do you remember when we were supposed to have brought in a poem that said something to us?"

"It was only a week ago," says Mrs. Hatcher. "Even my memory is that long!"

"And I got a zero because I had been to my uncle's funeral, but you said I could bring one later."

"You got a zero because you didn't have a poem," says Mrs. Hatcher, "not because you had been to your uncle's funeral. In any event, you were to be allowed to make up the assignment."

"Yes, ma'am, I know. And now I've got just the most perfect poem."

Mrs. Hatcher smiles. "In that case, do share it with us!"

"Well," says Gloria, "the name of it is 'The Kiss,' " and everyone laughs. "And it's by Miss Sara Teasdale, and here it is: '*I hoped that he would love me, / And he has kissed my mouth, / But I am like a stricken bird / That cannot reach the south.*' " Everyone is smiling except Amanda; I watch her.

Gloria looks up from the book and asks, "Isn't that just the prettiest thing?"

"Read the rest of it," says Mrs. Hatcher.

"Oh, I am. That's the sad part. I mean the second verse is the sad part, not that I'm going to read it. I mean that me reading it is not what's sad."

"*My* reading it," corrects Mrs. Hatcher.

"Yes, ma'am, that's what I mean," says Gloria, starting to read again: " '*For though I know he loves me, / To-night my heart is sad; / His kiss was not so wonderful / As all the dreams I had.*' "

She closes the book, and some of us give her a round of applause. "Shh!" says Mrs. Hatcher, putting a finger to her mouth. "Yes, Gloria, the class agrees with you: that's *your poem.* And I'm delighted that you went to the trouble to find it."

"Yes, ma'am," says Gloria. "But don't you think the last verse was sad?"

"In a way," says Mrs. Hatcher, smiling, "but perhaps someone can think of a poem that will console you. Any suggestions?"

Amanda's hand goes up, and I am surprised. Of course, she knows that I put Gloria up to reading "The Kiss."

"I know a poem that might help her, Mrs. Hatcher," says Amanda. "It's called 'Child, Child,' and is by Sara Teasdale, too."

"Could you recite it for us?"

"I think I can remember the first verse: '*Child, child, love while you can / The voice and the eyes and the soul of a man; / Never fear though it break your heart— / Out of the wound new joy will start; / Only love proudly and gladly and well, / Though love be heaven or love be hell.*' "

"Splendid!" says Mrs. Hatcher. "Do you agree, Gloria, that there's some encouragement to be found in Amanda's poem for the disappointment found in yours?"

"Oh, I wasn't really planning to give up dating!" says Gloria, and the class laughs again. Soon a discussion is under way about other poems, and Gloria goes back to writing a note.

"Now let's pick favorites," suggests Mrs. Hatcher, and she asks which American poets we have enjoyed most. Robert Frost is the top favorite, but several girls like Emily Dickinson best. Four boys and one girl choose Edgar Allan Poe, and three boys pick Edwin Arlington Robinson. Mrs. Hatcher asks, "Is Walt Whitman anybody's favorite?" and two hands shoot up, mine and Amanda's. I start to take mine down, but it is too late. Mrs. Hatcher says, "Alan, could you come up with a Whitman selection that you especially like?"

"I like 'Animals,' " I say, and I begin to recite the poem, almost growling and looking straight at Amanda: " '*I think I could turn and live with animals, they are so placid and self-contained; / I stand and look at them long and long, / They do not sweat and whine about their condition; / They do not lie awake in the dark and weep for their sins.*' " I stop there.

"Very good!" says Mrs. Hatcher. "And you, Amanda?"

I am certain she will recite the love song from "Out of the Cradle Endlessly Rocking." I remember the opening: "*Shine! shine! shine! / Pour down your warmth, great sun! / While we bask, we two together. / Two together!*"

"I like 'Animals,' too," she says, and she begins quoting where I left off. She does it so well that it sounds as if she is merely saying how she feels about animals: " '*They do not make me sick discussing their duty to God; / Not one is dissatisfied—not one is demented with the mania of owning things.*' " Maybe she puts too much expression in that line, but then I remember her mother, The Housekeeper, and all those figurines.

" '*Not one kneels to another,*' " she continues, " '*nor to his kind that lived thousands of years ago; / Not one is re-*

spectable or industrious over the whole earth.' " She's speaking of her father now, Industrious Dad.

Walt Whitman may have written the poem, but Amanda makes it hers. Everyone in the class listens—even Rick Bledsoe, who sits looking at Amanda bug-eyed, as if she is talking directly to him. And Gloria stops writing her note to listen. I'll tell Amanda that she has performed magic. She should be an actress; she could out-dazzle anyone on Broadway! I'll tell her after school. Then I remember that I will not see her after school. We are no longer two together.

11

The Doldrums

Dad has worked out a swap—our house, with the extra acres of land, in the center of town, for a home in the new development. We went through the new house while negotiations were under way, but now the deal is final. "Oh, goodie!" squeals Daisy. "When do we move?"

"As soon as the electricians and painters have finished," says Dad. "It won't be long."

"Why don't we go over there," says Daisy, "and see what it looks like now that it's ours?"

Dad smiles. "It looks very much the way it did *before* it was ours, but we'll go over after a while. Let's wait for Irene." He goes downstairs to read the paper, and Daisy and I stay in the upstairs room. I'm helping her with grammar, but she doesn't stop talking about the new house long enough to think of homework. "I just can't wait to tell Nelda and Leona that we're moving," she says. "They're going to be pink with envy."

"Green," I say just as a catbird lights on the holly branch outside.

"A message from Buddy!" says Daisy. "You take it."

"Let me think. Oh, yeah, Buddy says tell us there's nothing so special about a new house."

"There is so!" says Daisy. "And he's not going to dampen my spirits one bit."

"Would you care to send back a message?"

"Yes," she says, turning to the bird. "Tell Buddy he's just jealous 'cause we're moving and he's not!"

I suppose Daisy is right: There's no need to take Buddy along. Yet it gives me a strange feeling to think about it. I realize for the first time that we really will be moving, that it's not just talk of something we'll never get around to doing. We'll leave our old house—and our old life—behind. I should be glad of it.

The catbird flies away, and I stare in the direction it has flown, thinking of all the years we've played the game about Buddy. It will be different without him. Just then Dad calls from downstairs: "Come on, Alan! Daisy! Irene's here. Let's go over to the new house!"

At the end of English class Gloria hands me the Teasdale book. "I forgot to give this back to you yesterday," she says. Then she whispers, "There's a note in it." Evidently she has decided to use me as her postman. I'll deliver the note this time, but if she tries it again I'll explain that my help in canceling out her zero was purely a matter of aggravating Amanda. But while I am thinking this, Gloria smiles at me so warmly that I do not really mind if she thinks my help was offered out of concern for her. She's pink and pretty, and when our arms are pushed against each other as we start through the doorway I do not hurry to take mine away. "Who's the note for?" I ask.

"You," she whispers, and I am surprised—and excited. I do not know what to say and am glad when a group of sophomores comes between us.

At my locker I read the note and am disappointed. Although it is to me it is about Lanky. Gloria hopes that he will take an interest in her, and since Lanky and I are good friends she wants me to get the idea across to him. She thinks he would consider her too forward if she wrote him directly. According to her, she has often had crushes on boys, but this time she is absolutely certain that it's real love.

Lanky arrives at his locker, which is next to mine. "Gloria thinks you're quite a guy," I say. "She's going to be at Stumpy's with some of her pals after school, and if you want to take her home afterwards, buddy-boy, it's up to you."

"Yeah, I'll bet!" From the way he laughs it's obvious that he thinks I'm kidding.

"I guess she must have used up all the seniors," I say, "and now she's dropping down to us juniors. And Lanky-baby will be first!" Lanky still thinks it's a joke, so I hand him the note. "She's going by height," I say. "I'll be next!"

He reads the note quickly and says, "Well, Christmas morning!" grinning as if it were. Handing the note back to me, he shakes his head as if he still doesn't quite believe it. "I guess it's my charm!" he tells me.

"It's your driver's license," I say, "and your father's car." Lanky's father lets him use the family car after school whenever he wants it. "Enjoy your turn," I say. "Comes June I'll get my license, and you amateurs will have had your day!"

He laughs as we start into homeroom to wait for the final bell. "Well, here goes," he says. "Loss of innocence!"

At home I am alone in the upstairs room. I try to study geometry but can't keep my mind on it, so I pick up the literature book. I consider skipping tomorrow's assignment, "History of American Drama," and reading the first play instead. I hate introductions but have always felt duty-bound to read them. I have finished four pages when I realize that I do not know a word I've read. My mind is on Amanda. I think of her with Hap and am angry.

I turn to the first play; maybe it will distract me. But I continue to think of Amanda. I wonder if she is parked in front of the drugstore with Hap. Or maybe she's at Stumpy's with him. Still worse, maybe he's giving her a driving lesson. The thought hurts me. Outside Ellenville, except for the highway to Atlanta, roads are quiet and peaceful. I visualize Hap and Amanda riding along one of them. There are pastures and woods and rolling farmland ready for spring plowing. They turn onto a side road and stop at the edge of a tree-shaded lane and walk into the woods to hunt "jugs," the flowers of the wild ginger. Or maybe they search for bloodroot, one of the earliest wild flowers to bloom here. It's a favorite of mine and Amanda's. Last year we found a stand of it and painted each other's face and arms with the orange red juice that flows from its stems. I can see Amanda close enough to Hap to use the Indian paint of the stems. She stands facing him, both her arms up as she works out an intricate design on his forehead. Then his arms go around her, and they forget about bloodroot. It gives me a sick, empty feeling, and I remind myself that it's only what I imagine, not what's happening. Not *necessarily* what is happening.

An hour later I am still staring at the play, having read

no further than the title, *Where the Cross Is Made,* when the front door opens and someone starts up the stairs. "It's Amanda!" I say to myself. "It's got to be Amanda!" as the door opens and Irene enters.

"Where've you been?" I ask. "I thought you'd be coming straight home from school."

"Why?" she asks. "I'm not in mourning. Liz and Cathy invited me to go with some of the crowd out to Stumpy's, so I piled in and went along." Liz and Cathy are the Dalton twins, friends of Irene's since first grade. Their uncle owns Stumpy's, a combination country store and swimming lake, with a big dance pavilion on the back of the store. In the summer a band from Atlanta plays on weekends, and the place is crowded with out-of-towners. Off-season, it's a good place to drink Cokes and listen to the juke box.

Irene goes through a stack of records. "I'm not sure but what it's more fun to be with the crowd than to go steady," she says. "We had a good time, and Cathy taught us a new jitterbug step. Here, let's put something faster on, and I 'll show you." She punches the reject button on the record player, ending "I Hear a Rhapsody," and puts on "Rhumboogie." While it plays she does the wildest-looking step I ever saw. When the record ends she flops into a chair. "Guess who else was at the lake?"

"Hap and Amanda?"

"No. Your friend Lanky, with Gloria. Did you know they were going together?"

"I arranged it."

"Hap and Amanda weren't out there, but I saw them in front of the drugstore when I started home."

"Did you speak to them?"

"Why sure! I was walking that block. Liz and Cathy had stopped at the beauty shop to wait for their mother to finish work, so I walked the rest of the way home. Hap and Amanda couldn't help but see me, and they couldn't help but know that I couldn't help seeing them."

"That's a lot of *couldn't helps*," I say, willing to change the subject.

"I didn't go out to the car and chat, if that's what you mean. But I waved and kept right on going." She begins to sort records, then adds emphatically: "And that's what I intend to do: keep right on going!"

"You don't seem to mind that you've lost Hap."

"I'm not certain I've lost him. Who knows? He may miss me more than he thinks he will."

"And you'd forgive him and take him back?"

"I'd forgive him whether I took him back or not. I believe in forgiving anybody who wants to be forgiven, don't you?"

"I hate 'em both!" I say angrily.

"I don't hate either one of them," says Irene, putting a stack of records on the player. "Sure, I'm more upset than I admit, but God knows we've all had practice in putting up a good front." She is referring to Mom's absence, and instead of commenting I start reading *Where the Cross Is Made*.

"Oh, well," says Irene, "I kept Hap longer than anybody ever has. And too, I might have had to send him on his way pretty soon."

"Why?"

She looks at record labels instead of me. "Well, he was beginning to want more than I was willing to give him. We were getting serious, and he was too persistent in some things. About *one* thing, to be honest—and I chose not to give in. So maybe it's just as well that I'm rid of him."

"Maybe so," I agree, starting again to read the play.

"And now it's Amanda's turn. Do you think she'll give him what he wants?"

I pretend to be so caught up in reading that I do not hear.

12
The Move

On the second Wednesday in April we move into the new house. School is closed for a teachers' meeting, so Daisy, Irene, and I are home. Dad has taken the morning off, and he has hired Big Hal, the local moving man, to help us. My friends Blake and Lanky are helping too, and Blake has his father's pickup truck.

Mid-morning, after we've loaded the dining-room furniture onto Big Hal's van, we put Daisy's piano onto the pickup, along with two boxes of kitchen utensils and a blanket chest. "See you over there," says Dad, closing the tailgate. "Big Hal and I will grab another chair or two and be right along." Daisy and Irene are at the new house already, waiting to tell us where to put things.

On the way Blake drives as if he is in a race. We round a curve and come onto a washout in the road. Swerving to miss it, the truck almost turns over. We remain upright, but the piano does not. It is thrown off balance during

Blake's quick maneuvering and topples from the pickup. We are lucky: It lands in soft dirt on the shoulder of the road and stays there. If it had flipped over, or slid two more inches, it would have gone down a steep embankment and broken to pieces.

Big Hal and Dad arrive as we are struggling to get the piano back onto the truck. They stop to help us, and Big Hal says, "I nearly turned over the first time I came along here."

"It's a bad spot, all right," says Dad.

When we are under way again Blake says, "I'm glad your dad thought that was a dangerous place in the road."

"It is a dangerous place!"

"I know, but it wouldn't have been as bad if I hadn't been driving so fast." Then he laughs. "I guess I got excited over all the good stories Lanky was telling us about Gloria."

All three of us laugh. Just before the accident Blake and I had been asking Lanky about his romance, but he had refused to tell us anything except that Gloria is cooperative. He changes the subject now: "We're lucky the piano landed where it did. If it had gone down that bank, it would have wound up a high-priced pile of kindling!"

I picture it clearly, the three of us going into the new house with an armload of scrap wood, a stretch of ivory keys showing here and there, and asking Daisy, "Where do you want your piano?" It had been her Christmas present two years ago, and when she sees it now, a bit of mud on it after its ride across town, she complains loudly. None of us tells her it has taken a spill, although Big Hal teases her: "I think the boys drove *it* over here instead of the truck!"

Throughout the day, whenever Daisy is not around, he makes jokes about the accident. His favorite—he has repeated it three times—is "The piano zigged when the truck zagged." He laughs each time as if he's a great comedian. I could do without the humor.

After lunch Mr. Melton, who works with Dad at the appliance store, comes to help. Since the store is closed on Wednesday afternoons, he has brought along the delivery truck and a part-time handyman. By late afternoon the move is completed, and Dad says that he will treat the volunteer workers to a barbecue at the overhead bridge. He invites Big Hal to join us, but Big Hal declines, saying he'd best eat at home and get to bed early. "Tomorrow is a new day!" he says as if he's telling us something we'd never have guessed.

Breakfast the next morning is a bowl of cereal. We are not at home for lunch, so supper is our first big meal in the new house. Dad says grace: "We thank Thee, Lord, for these and all Thy many blessings."

I add, "Especially the double sink!"

"Thank you, Alan," he says, "for paying tribute to our new luxury!"

I think of Mom and wonder what she would have done on the first day here. She would have thought of something special. Whenever there was anything new at the old house, there was always a celebration. The first night after the back porch had been screened in, she had prepared all sorts of good things to eat, including deviled eggs and fried chicken. Beach towels were spread on the porch floor, and we sat on them and picknicked. Amanda had stayed for supper; Mom had always included Amanda in family parties. And there was the time the wash basin in the bathroom had been replaced; even that had been a special event. Mom had put ice cubes in the new basin and filled it with punch, serving goblets of it to Irene, Daisy, Amanda, and me, adding bourbon to the glasses she poured for herself and Dad. If she were here now, the first meal in our new dining room would be a banquet.

It is weeks before the house begins to look as if anyone really lives in it. Miriam has straightened the kitchen and then begun a floor-waxing and window-cleaning campaign that occupies her time. Dad has not insisted that anything be done in a hurry. Every night after supper he and I lift furniture while Daisy and Irene suggest where to put it. We all but wear out some of the pieces in shoving them around. Eventually things begin to settle into place.

I do not worry how my room looks. On moving day I shoved boxes into my closet, planning to unpack someday. When the weather begins to get hot and Daisy can't find her bathing suit, she insists that every box in the house be checked. I finish unpacking but do not find Daisy's swimsuit. It turns up among dish towels in a kitchen cabinet.

Gradually I feel at home here. No ghosts! I think, remembering how Mom used to say she wanted a house that did not remind her of the past. During the last six weeks I have studied in my room or the den—or in Irene's room, where we've put the record player for the time being. Here it is easier to keep my mind off Amanda than it would be in the upstairs room at the old house. We have not come here together every afternoon since sixth grade. But I miss her, no matter where I am, although I do not admit it to anyone. I see her every day, but we are like strangers.

I notice that she begins to look unhappy. She seldom smiles, and often she does not pay attention to what is going on around her. One day she does not hear Mrs. Hatcher call on her, and when the bell rings she does not move from her desk. I go back into the room, and she and

I are alone. She sits staring out the window. Standing in back of her, I ask, "Didn't you hear? The period has ended."

She looks at me as she gets up. "Oh, hi, Alan. I didn't realize the class was over."

"Are you all right?"

She runs one hand through her hair. "Oh, sure, I'm fine." She smiles at me as we go into the hall. "What about you? Are you all right?"

"I'm able to hear the bell when it rings," I say. "I thought for a minute you were dead."

"Not yet," she says, stopping at her locker, and I go ahead to mine.

On the last day of school I take my geometry final. Seniors have taken their exams early and have spent the past two days rehearsing for graduation exercises that are to be held tonight. The rest of us have had to work until the last day. I turn in my math paper and go home soon after lunch. A few minutes later Irene runs into the house. "Come ride to Atlanta with me," she says. "Hurry!"

"What for?"

"We unpacked the decorations and everything for the farewell party, and the favors weren't there." Irene is chairman of the social committee for the seniors, and their farewell party is being held tonight after graduation. "They're the main things," she continues. "Liz and Cathy are going to do the decorating, and I've got to go to Atlanta to pick up the favors. Dad's letting me use the car if you'll go with me."

"Why doesn't Hap go? He's on the social committee." Irene had appointed him early in the year.

"He's out at Stumpy's with the crowd. After we finished

the last rehearsal, 'most everybody went out there. Liz and Cathy and I were going to decorate the lunchroom for the party; then we were going to the lake too, but now this has come up. They're doing the work while I go to Atlanta."

En route to Atlanta Irene asks, "How'd the geometry go?"

"Not too bad. I think everybody passed."

"Even Gloria?"

"Gloria doesn't take geometry, but she's in my English class, and I expect she made pretty good. When she realized that literature can be fun, she began studying."

"Wouldn't it be funny," says Irene, "if she made a better grade on it than you or Amanda?" Usually Amanda and I make the top grades in our classes.

I laugh. "She may have made better than I did, I don't know, and I'm certain she made better than Amanda. Everybody in the class probably made better than Amanda."

"What? Has being in love caused her to quit studying?"

"Something has. For a little while after she and Hap started going together she was sharper than ever, but during the past few weeks she hasn't listened to half of what Mrs. Hatcher has said or seemed interested in anything."

"Then I may be doing her a favor if I take Hap back—if he's going to cause her to fail."

"Oh, I think she did so well the first part of the year that she won't fail."

"Well, being in love with her hasn't hurt Hap's grades. He's continued to study, and I'm proud of him. He's going to graduate and go off to college."

"Maybe he'll take Amanda with him," I say disgustedly.

13
Voices in the Night

Dad calls the end of the house that he and I share "the men's dormitory." My room is toward the street, and a bathroom connects it to Dad's. He calls the master bedroom "our room," as if Mom will return home at any time. Daisy and Irene have rooms at the opposite end of the house and the living area is in the middle. The first time I notice even a small drawback to the arrangement is late at night after graduation: Irene's bedroom is too near the front door.

Earlier in the evening Dad, Daisy, and I had gone to see Irene graduate, and afterwards the three of us went to Griffin. Daisy had begged to go somewhere—anywhere. She had reminded Dad that he hadn't taken us for a ride at night in a long time. Mom used to persuade him to take us often. She especially liked such outings; so did Amanda. After graduation exercises, Dad agreed with Daisy that we should stay out longer. He said we were too dressed up to go directly home, anyway, so we rode to Griffin in the moonlight, drank sodas at the drugstore that offers curb service, and came home.

Dad went directly to bed, and Daisy started listening to "Public Defender" on the radio. One of the big things about vacation for her is staying up as long as she pleases and listening to late-night programs. I do not care for them, so instead of staying in the den I came to Irene's room, put records on the player, and stretched out on the bed to listen. I planned to stay awake, but instead I drifted into such a sound sleep that now, when voices outside wake me, I cannot remember where I am.

Half-asleep, at first I suppose that the conversation is coming from the filling station. The station is closed at night, but people are always stopping to use the pay telephone outside it. But it was near our *old* house, I remind myself drowsily. Wooded lots surround us now. Then I realize that the voices come from the direction of the front stoop, and one of them is Irene's. I consider yelling, "Quiet down out there!" but I don't want to spoil her fun on graduation night. Also, I remember that I am in her room. If she knew she was disturbing anyone she would move somewhere else to talk. She's saying now, "A full moon through pine trees! What could be more beautiful?"

"You could!" someone says in a low voice, and I am sufficiently awake to recognize a line when I hear it.

Irene ignores the compliment. "This view is even grander when I think of the one I gave up. That horrible sign blinking like crazy!"

Whoever is with her laughs. Then he says, "If you really want to know what could be more beautiful, I've told you. You are!"

"Well, I should hope so! Anybody looks better than a sign that says ECONOMY GASOLINE, THE BEST BARGAIN IN TOWN."

"Aw, you know what I mean!"

I sit on the edge of the bed, thinking I'll go back to my room. I've never approved of eavesdropping. Then I hear Irene's friend saying, "I'm trying to be romantic, but you won't let me!" and I blink, suddenly realizing that it's Hap. In spite of my belief in other people's right to privacy, I remain where I am. "Aren't you glad to have me around?" he asks.

"If I weren't, you wouldn't be here," she answers.

"I'm being serious."

"Well, I'll be serious, too. I'm not as wild about you as I once was. Maybe someday I will be, who knows? Maybe you won't hang around to find out. It's as simple as that." Then she asks, "Wasn't Amanda upset that you didn't invite her to the farewell party?"

"I told her that mostly seniors would be there. Of course, she knew I was lying and that the other guys would bring their girlfriends, seniors or not, but she didn't object. I think she was glad I didn't ask her. She's been acting strange recently."

"How?"

"Oh, I don't know. Mostly she's no fun to be with anymore."

"So you've come back to me?"

"Look, do I have to get down on my knees and beg? All right, I will." There is a rustling noise, and then he asks, "Now, will you forgive me?"

Irene laughs. "Get up off your knees! You're making a hole in our new lawn!"

"You know," he continues, "you're the only girl I've ever asked to take me back. Until now, Good-time Hap kept moving on. But, yes, I do want to come back."

"On my terms?"

"Yes."

"But you'll hurt Amanda. Maybe you've already hurt her."

"I've helped her grow up," he insists.

"You've hurt Alan too."

"I hate it about him, I genuinely do. But if it hadn't been me, she'd have left him for somebody else."

"Maybe not. Still, maybe it's been good for all of us. None of us can take the other for granted anymore, and who knows but what Alan and Amanda will go back together? And who knows but what you and I will make a go of it this time? It's a chance I'm willing to take!" There is the clicking sound of the doorknob being turned. "Good night, Hap."

"Hey," he pleads, "don't go in yet!"

"On *my* terms, remember?"

"You win! I'll see you tomorrow. Sleep good without your neon sign!"

"Isn't it awful?" she says, sounding blissfully happy. "From my bed all I'll be able to see is the moon."

"Cheer up," he says, "maybe some clouds will blot it out!"

14
Amanda's Visit

I make toast and scramble three eggs, my usual breakfast on a Saturday. For a few days after school closed I was at home every day, not getting up till the middle of the morning, and Miriam cooked for me. She fried bacon to go with the eggs, but I do not go to so much trouble. Her breakfasts were better than mine, but I am glad that she is off on Saturdays. I do not have to listen to her complaints about my ruining eggs with catsup. Combining eggs and catsup is one of her many ideas of sin. I was glad when my summer job started because it keeps me away from home on weekdays. I earn money and am separated from Miriam at the same time. Lin Davidson and I have jobs with the construction company that is building a new school. I work for the brick masons.

Irene has a summer job too. This fall she will go to a business school, but now she is working at Beany's Dress Shop. Daisy does not have a job, but she spent last night with one of her friends and has not returned home yet. The house is especially quiet. No one else is here, and there are no traffic sounds and no clanging noises from a filling station. I like the silence, and I like Miriam not being here. I put more catsup on my eggs in honor of the occasion.

Later in the day I want to try out the new city swimming pool, so I go to my room after breakfast and rummage through the dresser until I find my swim trunks. I put them on to see if they still fit. They are too tight, a reminder of how much I've grown the past year, but they will do until I can buy another pair. I look at myself in the mirror and am proud of my physique. I will show it off at the new swimming pool.

The doorbell rings, and I answer it, still wearing the trunks. Amanda stands on the stoop. "Good morning," I say.

"Hi," she says, and when I say nothing else she adds, "I came over," as if I can't see for myself that she has.

"Who brought you?" I ask, noticing the shiny red Ford parked out front.

"Nobody. I drove myself." She attempts to laugh. "Didn't you know, I have a car? My folks gave it to me."

"They didn't give Ellie one till she went away to college."

"I know. That's the way it was then. But this year the Bronsons and the Kilmers have given Marie and Bootsie cars, and since Marie and Bootsie still have one more year in high school, the same as Amanda Moore, well, Amanda Moore has a car the same as Marie and Bootsie!"

I smile. "Your folks have to keep up!"

"You know my mother! She talks about teenagers and how they shouldn't be turned loose with automobiles, so she made Dad buy one for me! Isn't that funny?"

"Real funny," I say, flatly.

"But the neighbors were doing it, and you know my mother."

"You've said that once!"

She looks as if I've hurt her, then she brightens. Pointing toward the car she asks, "Care for a ride?"

"No, thanks."

She shifts uneasily, still on the stoop. "But I didn't really come to show off the car. I wanted to talk with you."

"About what?"

"Aren't you going to invite me in?" she asks. I stand inside the screen door, propped against it.

"Sure, come in." I hold the door open.

As she walks past me she looks down at my swim trunks. They are a deep tan, almost the shade of my skin. "When you came to the door I thought for a second you had forgotten to put on any clothes!"

I pull at the band of the trunks. "I was trying these on when the bell rang." Suddenly I feel awkward. "They're too tight."

Amanda looks me up and down and does not seem embarrassed. "You're as handsome as ever—and bigger than you were last summer." If I can't tell that I've grown the past year, she doesn't need to let me in on it as if she's made some great discovery. In a minute she'll tell me that last year I didn't have hair on my belly, the part of it that shows, and I'll tell her it was only that the trunks had come up higher last year. I will not let on that I've paid any attention to the way in which my body has matured. We stand awkwardly inside the front door, and Amanda says, "I like your new house."

"This is the living room," I explain. Now I am the one

making dumb statements. She can see for herself that it is the living room. Pointing toward the den, I say, "It's more comfortable in there," and we go into the next room.

Amanda sits down, looking weary, and I say, "Usually people sort of bubble over when they get a new car. It doesn't seem to have that effect on you."

"No, I'm not bubbling over."

"Then you must be sad. Let me see if I can guess why?" I smile, but she does not. "Maybe another figurine got smashed to pieces at your house, and you've been unjustly accused of breaking it?" She says nothing, and I add, "Or maybe you've been *justly* accused? Maybe you've smashed up everything."

Amanda smiles weakly. "Not yet. But it's an idea!"

I am being too facetious, but I do not stop. "Give me one last chance. Are you sad because . . . oh . . . maybe because Hap has left you?"

"I don't miss him. And how do you know he's left me?"

"He and Irene are going together again." I force a laugh. "From that I somehow guessed that he's not going with you!"

"I didn't know he was back with Irene," she says. "I haven't been anywhere or seen anybody since school was out."

"Where've you been?"

"At home. Moping."

"Yes, I heard Hap say you weren't fun anymore." I know that I am smiling the way Daisy does when she thinks she has scored in an argument.

Amanda looks at me but does not smile. "You wouldn't be any fun either," she says, "if . . ."

She hesitates, and I finish the sentence for her: "If Hap

had left me for Irene? Oh, I don't know. If I had a new car I'd probably console myself by driving around until I found somebody new." I look at her angrily. Sarcastically I add, "And just for laughs, maybe I'd run by and speak to Alan. He's this kid I used to know, but he's a child really, and I'm all grown up. Why, I've dated Hap Jordan! I've really lived!"

Amanda has looked at me without saying anything until I finish. Then she says softly, "No, none of what you say is true. What I started to say was that you wouldn't be any fun either if you were . . ." She is hesitating again, and suddenly I feel sick. I know what she is about to say, even before she adds, "if you were expecting a baby."

"What? Are you kidding?"

"I wish I were."

"Is that why Hap left you?"

"He doesn't know. Nobody does. I haven't told anybody but you."

"Well, I *am* complimented! You go out and get yourself pregnant by some jerk and then come to me with the news."

"Hap's not a jerk. I don't love him. I thought I did, but I don't. But he's not a jerk."

"Then you picked a poor time to break up with him."

"Getting into this trouble was as much my fault as his. It takes two, you know."

Amanda is merely accepting her share of the guilt, but I act snotty. "No, I didn't realize that it did. You know how young and naive I am."

She ignores the comment. "I guess I didn't really want to keep from going too far," she says. "And we had fun together. He'd let me drive his car every afternoon, and, oh, please don't make me spell out every detail. One thing led to another, and—"

I interrupt her. "You got pregnant. You've said so already."

"Help me!" she pleads.

"How? By marrying you and becoming the father of Hap's baby? I'm almost sixteen, Amanda, and if I work hard all summer toting bricks for the new school, and if I don't spend everything I make sooner, by fall I'll probably have enough money to buy a record player of my own."

"No, I don't want you to marry me."

"Then what do you want?"

"You for a friend. Couldn't we talk, I mean really talk, the way we once could, and maybe somehow I'll get up the courage to tell my parents. Can you imagine what's going to happen? How do you think this will go over with The Housekeeper?"

"What about your father? He ought to help you."

"Oh, sure. He'll pay any bills I run up. If Mamma tells him to, he'll send me some place far off to keep down a scandal. The town's tired of the one your family has provided, so now it's the Moores' turn."

I want to say that maybe a day will come when people mind their own business instead of others', but instead I say, "Your mother had it coming to her!"

"No," says Amanda, shaking her head. "She's not responsible for what I did. Oh, she separated you and me; if she hadn't we might still be together."

"If you hadn't wanted to let her separate us, she couldn't have."

Amanda is surprised. "I suppose you're right. But still, she didn't force me to date Hap, and nobody forced me to do anything against my will. I won't add to my troubles by lying to myself about who's to blame." She waits for me to say something, but when I do not she goes on: "But it will hurt Mamma, and maybe Dad, too. But he'll only do what he's always done—pat me on the head, give me some money, and go to his office. Unless someone there mentions my predicament, it may not cross his mind again." She laughs as if something is really funny. "Can't you see him sitting at his desk and his secretary saying: 'I hear one of your daughters is in trouble,' and without looking up he'll answer, 'Now that you mention it, I do recall hearing something to that effect at home. It was my younger daughter, I believe, but she was always doing foolish things. Why, once she brought rolls to the table in a silver tray when there was no one there but some ragged-ass boy she was trying to impress.' " As if recalling the incident assures her that she cannot expect real understanding from either of her parents, she begins to cry. Tears run down her cheeks, and her voice breaks when she says, "I was always able to talk with your mother. I wish she were here now."

"I don't!" I snap. I have said it so often that it comes as a reflex.

Amanda looks up. She wipes the tears away, and her voice is almost steady as she says, "Don't forgive her, Alan! Don't ever forgive anybody for anything, do you hear?" Now *she* is being sarcastic. "You don't want to understand," she adds accusingly. I want to say that maybe I don't but I'll try. I should tell her that all our years together count for something, but instead I turn and stare from the window till she begins to laugh. It's a hysterical kind of laughter. "This is a big joke on me, don't you think?" she asks. "It's the very thing we thought would happen to Gloria Mason. Remember all we said about poor old Dr. Mason pointing the shotgun? Well, maybe it serves me right! I used to think I was above it all." When I still do not turn from the window she says, "*We* were above it all—you and me."

I turn to her, but she continues as if she must finish what she has started: "Well, you're by yourself now. You're the only one who's perfect." Her voice breaks slightly, and tears well up in her eyes again, but she rushes on: "You're still above it all! Well, lots of luck!"

She gets up and starts from the den, I follow her through the living room and out the front door. She makes her way down the walk, looking back at me. She is half stumbling—talking at the same time. "You stay above the crowd, do you hear? Just go through life being perfect and don't ever have anything to do with anybody who isn't, and if anybody ever disappoints you, just say to hell with 'em and keep going, do you hear?" She is almost shouting, although I am only a few steps in back of her. "And don't forgive anybody or forget anything or be willing to start over. Don't think for one minute that you'll ever make a mistake or do anything wrong!"

She turns and runs to her car.

15

Summer and Fall

I do not see Amanda again, which is all right with me; I hate her. But my friends worry because she stays at home all the time. Blake asks, "Why don't you call her? Why don't you get her to come swimming Saturday afternoon?"

"Why don't *you*?" I snap, and he makes no more suggestions.

A couple of weeks later Rick Bledsoe asks me the same thing, and when I tell him, "Why don't *you*?" he says, "I did. I called her, but she wouldn't come out with me."

At the pool, Bootsie Kilmer and I are propped against the railing for the high diving board. She says, "I've tried over and over to make Amanda get out of the house this summer." Bootsie lives next door to the Moores. "Maybe you could persuade her to be sociable, Alan." Without waiting for me to say anything she rattles on: "I don't know what's come over her."

Sue Elkins, stretched out on the platform across from

us, says, "You don't think Amanda's grieving over Hap, do you?"

Lanky steps onto the diving board. "Amanda's got more sense than that! You ought to call her, Alan." He does a back flip into the water before I can tell him to mind his own business.

At home I am given the same advice. Irene keeps reminding me that Amanda was my friend for a long time. "You should stay in touch with her," she says. "I've forgiven Hap for his fling with Amanda. I've forgiven him for everything." She does not know what *everything* includes.

Once she even drags Hap into a discussion with me. Dad and Daisy were listening to the Judy Conova program in the den, and I had moved into the living room to read. I was stretched out on the sofa when Irene and Hap came in. "Hap agrees with me that you should visit Amanda," says Irene, as if I were waiting for his approval. "Yeah," says Hap, "won't you drop by the Moores' just for old times' sake?"

"No," I say emphatically.

Irene shrugs and starts from the room. "I'm going to make us a pitcher of lemonade."

I think of leaving too, but instead I lie there. It's being childish, I know, but I tell myself that this is my living room as much as anyone else's. So I continue to read. After a few minutes Hap says, "I know how you feel, Alan."

I put down the book and glare at him.

"Look," he says, "I'm sorry. I know you hate me for coming between you and Amanda, and I don't blame you. But things like that happen." When I say nothing he continues: "I didn't set out to break you up, whether you believe me or not. Who can say why anybody suddenly starts liking somebody else?"

"Nobody," I say disgustedly.

"It all started the night we went to see *Gone with the Wind.* And later, well, one thing led to another."

That's what Amanda had said, "One thing led to another." But Hap doesn't realize that I know what it eventually led to, and he doesn't know that Amanda is pregnant. He adds, "For what it's worth to you, I think she missed you. In fact, I know she did."

I get up and start from the room. "Tell Irene I don't want any lemonade," I say before banging the door shut. I wish everybody would leave me alone about Amanda.

Soon I have my wish. No one urges me to call or visit Amanda, because she has gone to Sante Fe, New Mexico. Her aunt and uncle live there.

"Looks like she'd have gone to see them before summer was nearly over," says Marie Bronson. "Why, she'll have to turn around and come home before she gets out there good. Doesn't she know that school starts Monday?"

I know that Amanda will not be returning to Ellenville soon, so I am not surprised on the second day of school by Bootsie's report: "I called the Moores last night and asked if Amanda had gotten home, and Mrs. Moore said Amanda's going to stay in Sante Fe."

"Why?" asks Nettie Veal, sitting across from us.

"Because of the rheumatic fever she had that time, I guess," says Bootsie. "Mrs. Moore said Amanda hasn't been too well lately, and they think she'll be better off there. New Mexico has a good climate."

"*Georgia* has a good climate," I say just as the bell rings.

After supper when I am spreading out my books to do the day's homework I think about the start of other school terms. Amanda and I always had fun talking about new schedules, courses, and teachers. The beginning of school was an exciting time for us. Last fall when we were flipping through textbooks and talking about the prospects for the term, Amanda had been especially happy. I can hear her saying, "Just think! Next year we'll be seniors! Won't that be great?"

Well, I am a senior this year, and no, it is not great. I open my literature book and start to read, but I cannot concentrate on the lesson. It is impossible to keep thoughts of Amanda out of my head. Finally I slam the book shut. Homework and Amanda can take a flying leap.

Irene, across the table from me, looks up. Pointing at the book, she asks, "Who do you have for English?"

"Mrs. Bailey. She says we don't know grammar as we should and she'll concentrate on it."

Irene laughs. "She says that to every class!"

"Today we went through poems defining parts of speech," I complain.

Irene laughs again. "You'll be amazed at how many pronouns there are in this world. Still, I'm not sure but what they're more interesting than debits and credits." Irene is taking a business course. In the evenings she divides her time between studying accounting and writing to Hap, who is at the University of Florida.

In the evenings, after school is a few weeks under way, I do little more than help Daisy with beginning algebra. Otherwise I listen to records—or read, when I come across anything I like. Occasionally a novel holds my interest. I seldom bother to study, and by late fall my grades trouble Dad. According to him, I do everything halfheartedly now. "It's as if you've quit caring about anything," he says, holding up my report card for November. "Is something the matter?"

I mumble that nothing's wrong.

"Does basketball take up too much of your time?" he asks. He has been proud of me for making the team, although I have not distinguished myself as a player. He knows as well as I do that basketball does not take up too much of my time. I consider the matter closed, but he does not. He talks about wishing that he knew what to do. He says that he loves me enough to keep trying to help me. I love him too, but I do not try to help myself.

At school I am called into the office on the first Friday in December. Mr. Goodwin is at his desk. "It saddens me, Alan, when a student doesn't come up to what I know he can do." He shuffles a handful of papers. "Your grades until this year are proof of what you're capable of doing." He talks about the record I've made till now. "If you'd try you could be top student at graduation," he says. Then, holding up a list of new grades, he adds, "But look at these! It's as if you're giving up."

I consider telling him, "I'm giving up." Instead I promise to do better. The promise rests lightly; after school I do not even carry books home to study.

I play basketball Friday night, and our team wins. Coach Wilkins thinks we will become champions. Rick Bledsoe is the champion. He is the best basketball player Ellenville has ever had. The rest of us support him.

On Saturday I clerk at Colby's. Two employees have resigned, and Mr. Colby has asked me to take my old job back until after Christmas. I give customers their right change and get through the day with the enthusiasm of a sleepwalker. It is Sunday that I am jarred awake. The whole country is stunned. Japanese planes have dropped bombs on Pearl Harbor, and the United States is at war.

The following week my friends and I talk of enlisting,

but for most of us it is only talk. At our age parental consent is required, and our parents consent for us to remain in school. Rick Bledsoe, who is a year older than most of us, turns eighteen on the thirteenth of December and enlists in the Navy the same day. With him go our chances of being basketball champions, but it does not matter. Two days later we are told that basketball has ended, anyway. Because of the war and gasoline shortages, schools in the district have curtailed programs that require unnecessary travel. Coach Wilkins joins the Marines.

The war has strange effects on people at home. Dad goes to Alabama two days after Christmas and returns on New Year's Eve, bringing Mom with him.

16
The Return

"I told you so!" says Daisy.

"Told me what?"

"That Mom was coming home."

"You told me so," I say. "And you've told me that you told me so a couple of hundred times."

"You just can't take being wrong," she says huffily. "You said she wouldn't come back, but she did. I said all along she would. I told you so!"

Mom has been at home a week, and Daisy is overjoyed. Dad is happy too. He laughs more than he has for months. I am glad he is happy, but I do not forgive Mom for what she has done to him and to us. I avoid being around her much of the time. Some days we see each other only at meals. The house is big enough that I can be alone whenever I choose.

Daisy complains at supper, "I don't have any homework tonight, and there's nothing good on the radio." She is not allowed to listen to any of her programs if there is homework to be done.

Mom laughs. "That doesn't seem fair, does it? I know what let's do. Let's play cards!"

"Yes!" squeals Daisy. "I'd forgotten about card games."

"Me too!" says Dad, getting up from the table. "I'll go find the cards."

"Let's play hearts," says Irene, "so all of us can play."

The whole family has gone crazy. Mom is delighted that her idea has gone over so well. It's as if she has rescued the household from some terrible fate instead of merely suggesting a card game because Daisy has no homework. The house is filled with a festive atmosphere.

I get up from the table, and Mom asks pleasantly, "Won't you join us?"

"I've got other things to do," I say. She looks hurt, and the festive atmosphere vanishes. No one says anything as I start away.

Dad, coming back into the room, asks, "Aren't you joining in?"

"No, thanks."

"Too bad!" he says good-naturedly. "You'll miss the fun."

Later, from my room, I hear everyone laughing. Perhaps someone has been caught with the Queen of Spades and all the hearts but one. That can be a laughing matter.

In mid-January I think of Amanda often in spite of myself. I have added nine months to the short time that she and Hap were going together, and I know that the baby is due in January or February. I stand at a window in the den, staring out, wondering how she spends her time while waiting for the baby to arrive. I wonder if she has read

Grapes of Wrath or *For Whom the Bell Tolls,* my favorites of the few novels to catch my interest this year. I wonder if she reads poetry. I wonder if she ever thinks of me.

"You look sad," says Mom. She is dusting bookshelves along one wall. I had not realized that anyone had come into the room. When I do not say anything she adds, "I miss Amanda," as if she knows what I'd been thinking.

"I don't!" I say angrily and leave the den.

In early February Bootsie Kilmer tells me that Mrs. Moore has gone to New Mexico. "I believe Amanda's sick or something," says Bootsie. "I believe rheumatic fever's set in again or something."

"Why do you think that?" I ask.

"Well, Mrs. Moore told my mother that she was going out to Sante Fe to be with Amanda for a week or two, sounding as if there were some special reason. But when Mamma asked if Amanda were sick, Mrs. Moore acted as if she wondered why Mamma would have gotten any such idea. 'Why, no, she's doing nicely,' is all Mrs. Moore said. You know how she can act—as if the Moores are not human like the rest of us."

A few weeks later while driving Daisy across town for junior choir practice, I see Mrs. Moore coming out of the shoe shop. Somehow I am relieved that she is back.

I return home to wait until it is time to pick up Daisy. In the den I read the current issue of *Life* and am glad that Mom is in another part of the house. Otherwise I would have gone to my room.

A moment later Mom comes into the den. I continue to flip through the magazine, although I glance at her. Neither of us speaks as she sits down. She picks up the afternoon paper, but instead of reading it she puts it back on the coffee table and looks at me. "I know you haven't forgiven me for what I've done to all of you."

"I didn't say I haven't."

"No," she agrees, "you didn't. But you and I have been so close over the years that sometimes we don't have to put everything in words."

"We're not close now."

She looks at me and continues: "Your father is happy that we're starting over. Maybe he and I have both made mistakes. And I'm glad to be back, but I wish you were glad to have me. We used to get along so well, you and I. Don't you remember?"

"No, I've forgotten."

A pleading tone comes into her voice, and she looks sad. "I know there's no turning back, that things are never the same as they were before. Still, I hope you'll consider what is past as being finished. Don't you believe in new starts?"

Before I can say whether I do or not a bluebird lights on a low branch of the tree outside. I must remember to tell Daisy. She and her scout troop are trying to turn Ellenville into a bird sanctuary. I recently helped her put up boxes that she said would attract bluebirds.

Mom says, "Why, I hadn't noticed! There's a low branch just outside, and it's a holly, isn't it?"

"Yes."

"My, isn't that a coincidence? It's exactly like the branch near the upstairs room at the old house." Then she laughs. "Look at the bird looking at us! Why, he's brought a message from Buddy! What does he say?"

I stare at her disgustedly. Hadn't she said a minute ago that things are never the same again? Then why does she expect us to continue playing some silly game as if nothing has happened? She looks at me, and I watch her smile fade away. A desperate expression replaces it. I start to say, "We've outgrown that stupid game!" but something stops me. I can hear Amanda, as clearly as if she were in the room, saying: "Don't forgive her! Don't ever forgive anybody for anything! Go through life being perfect and don't have anything to do with anyone who isn't. If anybody disappoints you, just say to hell with 'em! Do you hear?"

"I hear!" I say. "I hear!" Then I shake my head and am back to reality. Mom looks puzzled, almost frightened. It takes me a moment to think back to where we were before I *heard* Amanda.

I look at Mom and smile. "Buddy says tell us we only thought we could leave him behind." Even if things will never be the same, what harm is a game we've all once enjoyed? "Buddy says he was as tired of the filling station as we were."

"Where is he now?" asks Mom.

"Over there." I point toward the woods across the road. "Want to send back a message?"

"Don't you remember? Bluebirds and I don't speak the same language."

"That's right!" I say, turning to the window. "Go tell Buddy he had no business following us!" The bird flies away, and I call after it, "But tell him I'm glad he did!"

Mom laughs, and so do I. She reads the paper and I finish *Life*. We are comfortable in the room together, saying nothing.

17

Graduation and Gloria

At graduation I am not top student in the class, but I finish with honors. My friends and I are pleased to be out of high school. Lanky and Blake join the Navy the day after graduation. Both are seventeen already, and their parents have consented for them to go into military service.

The next person from Ellenville to enlist is Hap. At the end of his year of college in Florida he signed up with the Marines instead of waiting to be drafted. He will report for duty in two weeks. In the meantime he and Irene elope. There are many hasty marriages nowadays when men are at home one day and in the armed forces the next.

I try not to hate my brother-in-law. "Don't ever forgive anybody!" haunts me until I stop blaming him for coming between Amanda and me. Forgiving Hap is one thing; accepting him into the family is another. However, Irene cares so much for him that it does not matter what the rest of us think. When he leaves for boot camp, his parents invite her to live with them, but she returns home to be with us. After Hap has completed his training, she plans to follow him to whatever camp he is assigned to. Probably he will be sent overseas and she will remain in Ellenville for the duration of the war. *For the duration* has come to be a common phrase.

I turn seventeen in late June and decide to join the Navy. My parents decide that I will not. They want me to have a year of college first. I will not consent to that; college can wait until after the war. At the moment it is a standoff. I harp on the subject of going into service, and in an effort to get me to think about something else, my father allows me to use the car whenever I want it. Gas is rationed, but I do not need to take long trips. It gives me a new freedom to move around town behind a steering wheel.

When I see Roy Nelson at the drugstore on Saturday, he says, "I've got news for you. It's your turn."

"Huh?"

"Yep, Gloria Mason's interested in you."

"Well, that's a surprise!"

"I guess she figures you're the only one of us who'll be around for a while," says Roy. He has signed up for the Army Air Corps.

"Rub it in! I'd enlist if I could."

"Aw, I didn't mean you weren't doing your duty." He slaps me on the back.

I ask, "Do you suppose anybody has ever turned Gloria down?"

Roy laughs. "Who'd want to? I asked her why she picked you when I'm to be here for a few more weeks, but she said this isn't one of her usual flirtations. She says it's love!"

We both laugh, and he explains that Gloria is hoping I'll

pick her up this afternoon over at the swimming pool and take her home. Roy says, "Of course, it's just almost not possible to get from the swimming pool to Gloria's house without driving around back of the ball field and up one of those side roads and parking for a while to discuss things, if you know what I mean?"

"Innocent as I am, I know what you mean!"

In the afternoon I go for a swim and take Gloria home afterwards—by way of a lovers' lane. I have another date with her after supper, and we go to Stumpy's. She tries to teach me to jitterbug, although I do not care much for dancing. I go along with the lesson in order to get to the latter part of the evening, when we find our way to another lovers' lane. There she gives me lessons far more interesting than jitterbugging. She is a good teacher and I am a willing student. We get along well.

During the weeks since my first date with Gloria, she and I have been together often. I have a full-time construction job again this summer, but nights and weekends are for fun. I can't be with Gloria every minute as she has to be in by eleven so in the really late hours I hang out with Lin Davidson and Ned James. Their parents will not consent for them to go into the service either. After we've taken our dates home, the three of us get together and drink beer that we buy from a bootlegger. We sympathize with each other that we're not helping fight the war. We sympathize—and drink more beer.

My parents notice that I am later and later coming home. Probably they suspect that sometimes I am drunk. In mid-August they tell me they've changed their minds about my early enlistment: They'll give their consent.

I volunteer for the Navy before they can have second

thoughts, but the Navy does not want me. I am gravely disappointed. Earlier it crossed my mind that past leg injuries might present a problem, although doctors have assured me that both legs are all right. It is not my legs but my eyes that fail me in the examinations. Slight color blindness is detected. I have lived all my life without knowing that I cannot always distinguish subtle shades and tints.

"It's a sex-linked characteristic," explains a Navy doctor.

"WHAT'S THAT?" I ask, fearing that it is a price I must pay for the good times with Gloria. Perhaps I look as distressed as I have sounded.

The doctor laughs. "Don't worry about it. It's a trait, like bald-headedness, that a lot of men have but that's rare in women."

I say, "That's a consolation!" and go out and talk to an Army recruiter. The Army, it turns out, will be glad to have me, and I take papers home for my parents to sign.

On the day I am to report for duty I catch the bus into Atlanta. From downtown there are streetcars to Fort McPherson, but there is no need to rush. So I walk up to Peachtree Street and have a milk shake at Miner and Carter Drugstore. Then I go to the car stop.

A bookstore catches my eye just as the streetcar for Fort McPherson arrives. The conductor clangs the bell as if he is paid according to the noise he makes. As he calls "All aboard!" I step back. He scowls at me as if I am crazy to wait for a car and then not catch it. But an idea has come to me for one last thing I must do before going away.

Inside the store I ask, "Do you mail books?"

"Yes, certainly," says the saleswoman.

I will find something for Amanda, something I'm sure she'll like. First I look through the books at the poetry table, but none is certain to please her. I look next at novels. Spread out on one table are copies of *You Can't Go Home Again,* which I have read and enjoyed. Amanda would like it too, but the title is wrong for a gift to her now.

It is discouraging when nothing seems appropriate. Then, at a shelf marked SPECIAL EDITIONS, I see a copy of *Leaves of Grass.* Amanda and I have read it many times, but maybe she does not have her copy in Sante Fe. Also, this one, leatherbound, is unusually handsome; I must have it for Amanda. When I ask the price I regret that it has become a necessity. The price is more than I can afford, but I afford it anyway. I will skip milk shakes till an Army payday.

The saleswoman rings up the sale, and I give her the address that has been tucked in my billfold since the end of last year. Bootsie Kilmer had passed it out at school one day in the event anyone wanted to send Amanda a Christmas card.

I return to the car stop, thinking about the years Amanda and I could speak to each other through the words of a poet. Those days are gone, I tell myself, an old man of seventeen; they're part of my youth. Yet lines from the book I've sent her race through my head. They speak to Amanda for me now: "*O that you and I escape from the rest and go utterly off, free and lawless, / Two hawks in the air, two fishes swimming in the sea not more lawless than we.*" Another line all but shouts: "*What is it to us what the rest do or think?*"

"Right!" I say to myself just as a mighty clanging disturbs the morning. No longer a hawk in the air, I board the streetcar for Fort McPherson.